How the City Fell

Katelyn Prince

GLASSKO PRESS

GLASSKO PRESS

Glassko Press, Henderson, NV

www.Glassko.com

Manufactured in the United States of America

ISBN 978-0-9839640-3-2

Table of Contents

This book is dedicated to my father. He has supported me since this book was barely even a full idea and has helped me improve on it along the way. Thanks Dado!

N
W
E

Preface

The sorcerer walked down a cold, stone tunnel of the Underground Kingdom, his leather sandals echoing softly off the walls. All along the corridor phosphorescent moss that had been enhanced by magic cast an eerie, bluish-green glow everywhere he looked. A small smile twitched across his lips as he thought of the King's sorcerers, who had no idea where he and the Equalizers were hiding. He knew they would never discover that the Equalizers were within the island, right below their pampered feet. As he passed through a doorway, he slowed his normally fast pace, scanning the upper wall of the tunnel, until his eyes rested upon his target. A rune. Placing his hand directly below the symbol, he muttered the correct incantation, and the wall split. If he had been delivering bad news, he would have hesitated. But the news he was about to deliver was very good indeed. He walked through and the wall sealed behind him. Before him sat the Master of all Masters on his throne, looking out at the ocean which was held back by a shimmering wall, a magic spell.

"Yes?" the Master, Bacillus asked, his voice deep and serious.

"Sire," answered the first sorcerer, bowing low at the waist, "the Kale is in our possession."

Bacillus smiled, his lips a thin line. "Excellent. Has he answered any of the questions?"

"Not yet. But that will change after a few days with little food and water."

"Well done. Report to me if he says anything that could be of use."

"Of course, Sire," the sorcerer replied. "Do you have any further orders?"

"Yes, your apprentice Corvus is due for his final test."

The sorcerer looked up. "That is correct. Do you have something in mind?"

"Yes," Bacillus continued, stoking the fine velvet of his throne with his fingertips. "His final test will be to capture the princess, and bring her to me. Alive."

The Princess

"Throw it here!"

The moment she caught it, Princess Nicky threw the disk to Philo, a fellow team member. She and a few other children were playing a rather popular game that involved running, quick thinking, and keeping the disk away from the other team. Nicky looked around the circular Quibthrow court, brushing her long blond hair behind her ear. The court was laid out in the usual way for playing. The basket was in the center of a small circle. The circle was about three feet wide. Surrounding the circle were two half-circle arcs, each about four feet wide and three feet away from the circle. Surrounding those were two other half-circle arcs with a four foot gap and five feet wide. The circle and the half-circle arcs were painted blue. The space between them was red and the basket was brown and made of unused fishing net. As the disk traveled to the other side of the court, Nicky thought back to the first time she had played her now favorite game. It must have been about five years ago. She had been sitting in a nearby tree when a group of boys her age came by.

"Where're you going?" she had asked.

"To the new Quibthrow court!" one with black hair answered, stopping before the tree.

"What's Quibthrow?"

"It's the best game ever invented since the beginning of games themselves!" another boy exclaimed, this one with copper hair. "How come you've never heard of it?"

"Because she's a girl," the first boy stated. "Girls can't play games like that."

"I bet I could if you taught me how," Nicky stated.

"No you couldn't," the disbelieving boy scoffed.

"I could too!"

The boys looked around at each other. The black haired boy gestured for the others to lean their heads together and began whispering.

"This will take just a second," the copper haired boy informed Nicky. Nicky leaned forward to try to hear what they were saying, holding on to the branches around her.

When their whispering was through, the first boy, who must have been the leader of the group, said, "Alright, we'll give you a shot. But if you don't get the rules, you can't play."

"And if I do understand the rules?" she asked.

"Then you can play," he answered, though he didn't seem too enthusiastic about it.

Nicky smiled and hopped down from the tree. Over at the Quibthrow court, the boys laid out the rules.

"Alright, the goal of the game is this: if you're on the blue team, you have to get the disk into the basket, but you can only put it in if you're standing in the circle," one boy gestured to the area around the basket.

"Okay," Nicky had it so far.

"If you're standing somewhere else, you have to throw it to another team member, but you have to close your eyes."

"Close my eyes, got it."

Now the copper haired boy spoke, "Now if you're on the red team, the way you get points is by catching the disk or tagging a blue team member when they're running across the red area."

"If I'm on the blue team can I run while holding the disk?"

"No," the one with black hair spoke up. "I don't know why you would anyway; the red team would catch you for sure! Since, you know, your eyes are closed."

"Right," Nicky realized, "so blue team scores by getting the disk into the basket, red team by tagging the blue team or catching the disk. How many points do we play to?"

That depends on how many people are on each team," said the copper haired boy, "If there are five on each team, you play to five points. Ten on each, ten points."

"Okay, Anything else?"

"Oh yeah, my favorite part." The black haired one smiled. "The winning team gets to pick a penalty for the losing team."

"Like what?"

"Depends on who's on the team," the copper haired one said. "It can be anything from picking fruit for the winning team to catching a certain fish."

"Okay, blue team scores by getting the disk into the basket, red team scores by catching the disk or tagging the blue team, points depend on the number of players, and you want to win. *Anything* else?"

"Yeah," the one with black hair said, "you have to wear a sash of your team's color around your head." He handed Nicky a red sash, and she put it on. The rest of the boys decided who was where and the game began.

"Nicky!"

She snapped back into reality, just in time to snatch the disk out of the air. The moment she caught it she closed her eyes, keeping the location of where her team was in her mind. Yelling "Tasha!" she threw the disk to her good friend and fellow team member, who was standing in the circle. With a triumphant yell from the blue team Tasha scored a point, giving the blue team a score of ten, the amount needed to win. The nine other members of the blue team poured forward to congratulate her while the ten members of the red team started to line up and await their penalty. After the blue team had finished celebrating, one girl, Adella, turned towards the red team.

"Alright red team. It is my job as team captain to tell you what your penalty will be. So be nice while we decide and we might go easy on you." Adella smiled and stepped back and the blue team began to whisper amongst themselves. After what seemed like ages to the red team but in reality was only two minutes, Adella stepped forward yet again. "Okay. The blue team has decided that your penalty for losing is..." She paused dramatically as her face twitched into a small smile... "You have to go dive for clams right now and bring them back to us."

"How many?" asked Grenden, the red team captain.

"Two," she replied, then added, "you each have one minute, or you have to get three more clams. Go."

And with that the entire red team took off down to the water front and dove in. A few of the blue team members dove in just to cool off. One advantage to playing in the Trill's Bay was that both water and clams were never far away.

A little while later, the red team had finished their task and trudged up the white sand to where the blue team members were lounging in the shade.

"Here are your royal clams, *your highnesses*," said a soaking wet Grenden in a sarcastic tone. Then with a quick glance at Nicky he added, "No offense, Princess."

"None taken," she replied, taking a clam.

"Just be happy we live someplace where the water's warm," Adella stated.

"Oh, I'm not complaining about the temperature," Grenden replied, "It's the middle of summer; the shallow water is at least eighty degrees. I'm saying that getting clams was an easy penalty."

Adella tossed her auburn hair out of her face. "What do you mean?"

"Well, clams are so abundant here, that something worth being called a penalty would have to be hard."

"Really? If getting clams was so easy, why did it take you over the time limit to collect all of them? Hmmmm?"

Grenden decided to change the subject. "Speaking of clams, are you going to eat those raw?"

"Of course not," Adella replied, "Build a fire."

"What? Why me?" Grenden demanded.

"Because," she answered, "your team had to get us clams. If they got us clams, you should make the fire since we can't eat them raw. Besides, you should know stuff like this."

"That doesn't make any sense!" he exclaimed.

"It does too," she replied.

"To you maybe!"

"What's that supposed to mean?"

"Whoa, hey," Philo said as he walked up, throwing a small stone aside, "I just finished building a fire. Honestly, you two sound like you're betrothed or something."

Grenden and Adella glanced at each other, and then back at Philo. Philo looked around at the rest of the kids, finding that some were staring at him, though most seemed to have suddenly found common objects in need of intense studying. One kid was closely studying his fingernails, while a few others were scanning the trees.

"What?" Philo demanded at the staring kids, "Wait a minute. Are you two *actually* betrothed?"

When Adella nodded reluctantly Philo could not believe it. "Since when?" he spluttered.

"Since her parents want to know why our Uttapam tastes better than theirs," Grenden grumbled.

"And why our Mazo is lighter than theirs has ever been," Adella finished, "They're both kind of family secrets."

"I thought people were only betrothed to learn important secrets," one girl wondered aloud.

"Our families own bakeries," Adella responded with a sharp note to her voice, "Recipes are *very* important to us."

The girl muttered an apology.

After a slightly awkward silence, Tasha, the girl who scored the winning point, spoke up. "Um, can we start cooking our clams now?" she asked.

After a couple of murmured answers, the members of the blue team began grabbing various clams and cooking them.

A few of the dripping wet red team members plopped down on the powdered sand, staring at the clams being cooked and eaten. After both a game of Quibthrow, and collecting two clams in under a minute, they were all getting pretty hungry. Noticing this, Nicky started to offer one of her clams to a red team member when she was interrupted by Grenden.

"What are we doing staring at their clams?" he asked his team. "We can go get our own! I mean, we're already soaked." The rest of the red team nodded vigorously and a few shouted, "Let's go!" and they all took off yet again down to the water front for more clams.

"Honestly," muttered Adella, "if they wanted clams, why didn't they think of that while they were down there in the first place?"

"Wait just a minute," said Philo, turning to Adella. "As I seem to recall, last time you were on the losing side, you had to climb a monomak tree and collect, what was it, three berries each?"

"Ah yes, that's right," Nicky added. "And if I recall correctly, Addie, you did the exact same thing! Starring at the winners eating berries until one of your team members came down the tree with ten berries and shared the extras." Now everyone was staring at Adella, some not hiding their smiles as well as others.

"I was young and foolish then," cried Adella.

"It was last month!" exclaimed nearly half the team.

Before Adella could be reminded of more silly things she had done in her past, Tasha glanced up at the sun and asked, "Um, Princess Nicky? Weren't you supposed to be at the Palace by three o' clock?"

Nicky gasped as she glanced at the sky. "Oh no! I was! And that was at least twenty minutes ago!" Nicky jumped up, along with some other children who had lost track of time. Nicky looked around for Philo who usually walked home with her, since he lived very close to the Palace, but he had already left. Then, realizing she was wasting time, she sprinted towards the heart of the island.

Nicky loved the island she lived on: The green trees she would sometimes climb, the stone and clay houses with wooden roofs that her friends lived in, the dirt paths that were slowly becoming cobblestone roads, the wagons pulled by gazelle, cattle, and horses, the delicious smells from the various shops, and the green fields and hills that she would roll down when she was not late. But what had to be one of her favorite things was all the people that lived here, too. It was not an uncommon thing to see the Princess running through the outdoor markets or village square. Half the time she was playing running games, the other half she was late for one thing or another. She was a bit irresponsible when it came to keeping time. As she would run by the bread maker's house, his twelve year old daughter, who was two years younger than Nicky, would frequently run small loafs of bread to her if she came by near the noon meal time, also known as mid-meal. Nicky was kind of sad it was too late for mid-meal; she enjoyed talking with the bread maker's daughter. As she continued running, Nicky glanced up at the rapidly setting sun. She decided to take a short-cut. She locked her legs as her short-cut came up, turning her body while skidding, for maximum speed while turning. Even though cobblestone roads were much more efficient, since they were not dusty and did not turn to mud, she was grateful the shortcut had not been paved yet; otherwise her feet might have been scraped in her skid. She continued on like this, skidding between shops and dodging people that walked by, until she ran out of the marketplace and into a neighborhood. She was almost home.

Just as Nicky was nearing the Palace wall, she tripped, throwing her hand out in front of her just in time to avoid falling flat on her face. She rolled over on her back and, when her breath returned about a minute later, she pushed herself into a sitting position and inspected her hands and knees. Hands, a little scraped up. Knees, barely a scratch. She stared at the thing she tripped over, a toy belonging to a small child, who at that moment, ran out, swooped up the toy, and ran back into the house. Nicky shrugged and started to rise.

As she was standing, something caught her attention. Shading her eyes against the slowly sinking sun she squinted down the pathway. Coming down the road was a man in a long, dark cloak. As the man walked the cloak shimmered from one color to another so that, as Nicky watched, it changed from a dark purple to a midnight blue to a serpent green to coal black, then back to the dark purple. Nicky realized who this was immediately. A sorcerer. Nicky looked closer and realized that she had never seen this particular sorcerer before. And, as a princess, it was her duty to know each and every sorcerer that served under the King. If she did not know this sorcerer, he did not work for the King. And every sorcerer that Nicky knew that did not work for the King was serving under someone who was against the King. Nicky started slowly backing against the wall of a nearby house, hoping he had not seen her yet. She *was* the princess after all, and should probably keep her distance from anyone opposing the King. Before her back touched the wall someone pulled her through the open doorway! Nicky quickly spun around with a small gasp of surprise.

"Philo!" she exclaimed.

"Shhh."

He motioned her to stay down and crept towards the only window in the front room. Nicky followed. With their eyes barely peaking over the edge of the windowsill, Nicky and Philo watched as the sorcerer came closer. He was about twenty feet away when Nicky caught sight of another sorcerer from the opposite direction. But instead of a shimmering cloak of dark colors, this one's cloak changed from clover green to sky blue, to ruby red. She recognized this one as one that lived in the Palace, named Sefton, the apprentice to the Kale.

Ah, no wait. He had been graduated to full overseer of the Kale realm, Nicky remembered.

It was a moment before the first sorcerer noticed Kale Sefton, but when he did his face broke into a smile. A smile that had no joy or humor in it. A smile that was full of wickedness. His right hand disappeared deep inside his sleeve, which already came down to completely hide his palm. When his hand reappeared, it was holding a straight, smooth twig no longer then five inches. Kale Sefton had done the same. Philo took a sharp breath. Before Nicky could wonder why, both sorcerers raised their twigs up in front of their faces and began muttering the way sorcerers do. With a dark red glow, the first sorcerer's twig began to grow into a three foot staff made of dark elm wood, twisting around itself and complete with a violet gem embedded in the middle. Kale Sefton's twig also became a staff, his with an aqua gem at the top, the light oak staff braided over the gem to keep it in place. The courtyard was filled with a silence that came from every face in every window holding their breath. Nicky noticed Philo was rubbing his left hand, like it was in pain. She instantly forgot this though, for right then the sorcerer spoke.

"Ah! An apprentice," His voice reminded Nicky of a spider that had just caught a fly. "Bid me entrance to this realm." Then, as if an afterthought, he said, "How old are you anyway? Twenty? Twenty-two?"

"You know my answer, Volcanis." The young sorcerer replied, "Leave, and don't come back, not until you are once again loyal to the King. And I'm no longer an apprentice. I've graduated to sorcerer." After a moment he also said, "And I'm twenty-four."

"Really? And why is it that one so young has been appointed Kale?" Volcanis asked in a sly tone, completely ignoring the first part of the Kale's answer. "Did your level of knowledge in the ancient art deepen? Or was it just because you were the previous Kale's apprentice?"

Sefton's grip on his staff tightened. "What do you mean, just because I *was* the Kale's apprentice?" He asked through gritted teeth. "What do you know about the previous Kale?"

"Ah! A very interesting story, that one," Volcanis replied coolly, now with both hands on his staff, "It goes a little something like *this*." There was a blinding flash of light as Volcanis thrust his staff into the air. With a flick of his wrists the gem set in the middle of the staff was aimed at Kale Sefton. Rapidly, the blinding light gathered together, to create a glowing green orb, centered at the gem imbedded in his staff. The same green his cloak contained. When it was as big as Nicky's head, Volcanis hurled the orb towards his opponent. It flew with amazing speed. Twenty feet away, eleven feet away. Five feet. It was only two feet away from Kale Sefton when he acted. Slamming the end of his staff onto the ground, a translucent, sky blue bubble appeared at his gem, quickly encasing the sorcerer and stopping the orb from hitting him. However, the jolt caused by the orb hitting his shield jerked Kale Sefton back at least three feet. After he stopped sliding, he hurled three rapid beams of turquoise at Volcanis, who absorbed them with a shield like the Kale's, only this one dark purple. The sorcerer was also propelled backwards when the projectiles hit his shield, creating a slight trench in the unpaved portion of the road. The moment he recovered, he returned fire with dark red, translucent, glowing snakes. The duel went on like this for a while, beams and orbs flying back and forth, shields up just in time. Nicky looked around the courtyard. A few dents in a couple of walls where orbs had been misfired, and shallow trenches in the ground, not the usual damage one found at a sorcerer's duel of their level. She was just about to comment that their duel was not too intense, but immediately stopped. For just then, both sorcerers stopped firing and began circling each other.

"Why have they stopped dueling?" Nicky whispered to Philo.

"Nicky, they were never dueling, they were simply testing each other's strength," he whispered back.

Suddenly there was an explosion from outside and, as Nicky spun her head back towards the window, she discovered the sorcerer's duel was starting again. And this time, they were not testing each other's strength. Both sorcerers looked like they were standing on lava; they were jumping around, firing orbs, beams, glowing animals, and rocks, in a seemingly random pattern. Blue, green, red, yellow, pink, black, and so many other colors were flying back and forth it looked like a rainbow had shattered. With a flick of a staff, Nicky could not tell whose, a mini sandstorm engulfed the sorcerers. At first, nothing but the twister made any noise. Then, orbs, beams, and assorted glowing animals began flying in all directions. Nicky rose slightly from her kneeled position to get a better look at the orbs and rocks flying through doors and windows on the other side of the road. Just as it began to dawn on her that the pebbles the twister was kicking up were traveling at alarmingly high speeds, Philo grabbed her shoulders and threw her to the ground. A moment later a bright green translucent elephant slammed through the wall, walked a few paces, and evaporated, wood, glass, and dried mud flying everywhere. Before Nicky could stand, Philo grabbed her arms for a second time, and began dragging her away from the now destroyed wall. She scrambled to get her footing and, when she did, dove after Philo behind a wooden trunk. Once again on their hands and knees, Philo and Nicky were able to breath.

"Maker, keep him safe," Nicky murmured, her head turned to the sky. She heard Philo mutter a prayer as well.

Nicky thought the duel would never end when an explosion of light and sound shook the ground and rattled the walls of every building nearby. When the dust had finally settled, Nicky ventured a look around. The courtyard was in shambles, walls shattered, the road turned to dust, every door to every house reduced to splinters. Nicky hurriedly looked for the sorcerers. Volcanis had disappeared, magically transported to someplace where he escaped the explosion he had caused. Kale Sefton had not been so lucky. Nicky saw him, covered in dust and scorch marks, lying in a heap in the middle of a crater that must have been eight feet deep. Nicky started towards the doorway when Philo grabbed her.

"Philo! What are you doing?"

"Nicky it's not safe. What if that other sorcerer decides to come back and finish the Kale off?"

She was about to reply when Sefton stirred. With a groan he slowly began to raise himself to his feet.

Nicky breathed a prayer of thanks.

Leaning heavily on his staff the Kale reached into one of his many pockets within his cloak and pulled out a small pouch. Reaching in only his fingertips, he pulled out a small pinch of what looked like normal sand. Muttering strange words he threw the sand in front of him. But instead of falling to the ground, the sand stayed hovering in the air, slowly changing from a pinch of tan sand a glowing purple rectangle the height of a man. Painfully the Kale made his way through the rectangle and instead of appearing on the other side, he disappeared. After the Kale had completely disappeared, the doorway fell to the ground, once again normal sand. Nicky sighed in relief. She had seen sorcerers do this before. She knew he went somewhere safe and would get the care he needed. She turned back to Philo.

"You can let go of my arm now."

Philo let go, looking slightly redder than usual.

"Aren't you supposed to be home by now?" he asked.

"I AM!" she exclaimed and flew out the door. Before she had even passed the gaping hole where the window had previously been she was back.

"Why were you here in the first place?"

"My grandparents live here." He said in a matter-of-fact tone.

"Hmm!" she said. She then motioned to the wall with the hole big enough to climb through and said, "Sorry about that."

Philo shrugged. "The Nom will probably organize a team to fix everything. He is the realm overseer after all."

"Who do you think will help?" Nicky asked.

"Nicky! You have to go home!"

She slapped her forehead. "I know!" she groaned. She then took off towards the Palace, waving over her shoulder.

Philo waved back while laughing softly. "Some things just never change."

The Sorcerers

Nicky ran fast to the front gate of the Palace. Waving to the guards, she tore through the courtyard, the front garden and up the white marble stairs. When she entered the Palace she slowed to a quick walk so her bare feet would not slap against the marble tile. She did not want to attract too much attention since she was supposed to be home forty-five minutes ago. As she was nearing her chambers, she heard the small murmur of arguing voices. Nicky stopped to listen. The voices seemed to be coming from down the hall. Immediately forgetting the punishment that probably awaited her when her father discovered she was late, Nicky backtracked down the hall towards the voices. As she approached the voices, she realized that they were coming from the sorcerers' conference room, located in the very center of the Palace. Without the slightest hesitation, she peaked through the slightly opened wooden door. Eight feet from Nicky stood one of twelve pillars that stood in a circle, each two feet in diameter and eight feet from the next one. Between each pillar were two stairs going down to the middle of the room. On the floor were twelve lines, joined in the middle of the room and projecting out to the walls. If Nicky were looking at them from the ceiling, she would have been reminded of a mango pie cut into twelve even slices.

Around a central table sat all the king's sorcerers and sorceresses. Sitting at the table was Rus Nevik at the one o' clock position. At the two o' clock place was the Cor whose name was Ambris. Next was the Trill called Vowtiz, then Gar Coderious, Quen Anrym, Kale Sefton, Sem Tamaria, Tem Prisidious, Trune Sapphirell, Nom Drach , Mur Alana, and Bos Trenious at the twelve o'clock position. Then, looking closer, Nicky noticed that apprentice Trefton was sitting in Kale Sefton's place, although Trefton was the Gar's apprentice. This worried Nicky. Sorcerer council meetings were top priority. No one missed them unless they were on a mission or too injured to attend. That was one reason to have an apprentice. If a sorcerer was unable to make it to a meeting, his apprentice went in his place, and then filled him in later.

Rus Nevik was currently standing, saying something Nicky could not quite hear. Whatever it was, it sounded important. Nicky looked at all the sorcerers and sorceresses and, seeing that no one had seen her, slipped inside, pressing her back against the wall.

Once when she was in the village, she had been the only one to notice a mouse running along a wall, so small and light on its feet that anyone who was preoccupied would not have noticed it. Remembering that now, she made barely a sound as she eased herself to the floor. Then, lying on her stomach, she inched her way over to the nearest pillar and stood up, her back to it. Now she could hear what Nevik was saying.

"... Their move! I say we make ours."

"How do we know that they're behind both Kales' fate *and* the prophecy?" asked Tem Prisidious.

"We don't!" answered the Nom, Drach, "but we still need to warn the subjects!"

"If we warn the subjects, *they* will hear of it and abandon their mission!" exclaimed Bos Trenious.

"Isn't that what we want?" asked Trune Sapphirell. "For them not to attack us?"

Bos Trenious spoke in a tone one might use to explain to a toddler why he could not have a cookie. "Of course we do. But if they don't attack us after we raise the alarm the entire kingdom will think we're a bunch of crazy old paranoid goldfish who stare at crystal balls all day!"

Nicky giggled softly as the image of goldfish staring into crystal balls entered her mind.

"But they'd be safe." Sapphirell said in a small voice. It was common knowledge within the Palace that the Trune, Sapphirell, was intimidated by the Bos, Trenious, but hardly anyone else. Nicky was not sure why, but she figured the Bos's sharp tongue and the fact that he knew more spells then the Trune probably had something to do with it.

"And that's what we want!" Cor Ambris broke in, "the subjects to be safe."

Nicky could imagine the warning look Ambris probably gave Trenious. Even though he was older, Trenious listened to Ambris. Nobody really knew why.

"We're getting off subject," reminded the ever-practical Quen Anrym. "What are we going to do about the fall?"

Nicky could nearly hear the silence that followed. *What's the fall?* she wondered. Finally Legirious answered.

"Our number one priority is to keep our subjects safe."

"But how?" asked Sapphirell. "How will we be able to find and destroy Bacillus's sorcerers within six days?"

Six days? thought Nicky. *Why six days?*

"I don't know," replied Legirious.

"We need to figure out what the Oracle meant," Trill Vowtiz said at last. "What do we have so far?"

"We know that we can't trust anyone that we've already trusted," replied Gar Coderious, "Since 'conquered by enemy that had once been friend' is the first part of the prophecy."

Nicky's head swam. The Oracle had spoken? The sorcerers following Bacillus had made their move? The sorcerers still loyal to the king had to make theirs? The city betrayed by a friend? Nicky could not take any more. Just as she was about to sneak back out the door, the pillar she was leaning on vanished and, with the pillar no longer supporting her weight, she tumbled into the room in front of twelve sorcerers. Some surprised, some angry. Nicky, on her hands and knees, looked sheepishly up at the sorcerer standing before her.

"Princess Nickisha, what are you doing in here?" Rus Nevik inquired through gritted teeth.

"I..." she began. From a very young age, Nicky had been taught that lying to get out of a situation only made it worse. "I heard voices and was curious."

"As usual," murmured Trill Vowtiz and his sister Anrym nodded in agreement.

Nevik sighed. Although stern most of the time, the Rus had a soft spot for children. Especially Nicky, who most people liked almost instantly. "You do know you're not supposed to be in this room, correct?"

When Nicky reluctantly nodded, Nevik sighed. "I suppose I should call your father."

But before he had the chance the King himself burst into the room, "has anyone seen Nicky?" he asked. Then noticing Nicky he stopped in his tracks. "Oh," he said.

"Hi, Father."

"Well, thank you," he told the sorcerer council. Then, motioning for Nicky to follow him, walked out of the room. Nicky reluctantly followed out the door. She expected her father to start the questioning the moment the door was closed. But to Nicky's surprise, her father remained silent as he continued down the hall. Nicky realized that they were walking towards her father's private chamber. As their footsteps echoed on the walls, Nicky studied her father and was startled to find he looked worried. Her father was rarely worried about anything. Before she had any more time to consider it, they had arrived at the King's chambers. When her father closed the door, he sat on one of the many plush pillows covering the floor and motioned Nicky to do the same. Her father remained silent, sitting cross legged on his large, light blue pillow. He then picked up a scroll and began silently reading it to himself, giving Nicky the chance to look around. She was seldom in her father's private chamber, since it was usually only used when the King was seeking council from his advisers or debating a law with the sorcerers, who were the overseers of the realms.

She gazed at the high ceiling and dark wooden banisters that crept down to the floor. She stole a glance at her father. The dark haired man was tall and strong. He had defined features, and sad, grey eyes. Nicky sighed. Only those who knew him for a long time could see the suffering in his eyes. Nicky was content though. She knew of people who never laughed or joked after a loved one had died. She was glad her father still knew how to have fun, even though he had so much reason to be sad. With another sigh, she began to study the room again. Tapestries, scrolls on shelves, and an infinite number of stone doves, the symbols of wisdom. She had just finished counting the fifty eight of them sitting around the room when her father finally spoke.

"Three weeks ago today, Princess Nickisha was late to her music lesson by twelve minutes. Excuse: lost a game of Quibthrow and had to catch a live chicken."

Nicky turned towards her father and realized he was reading her tutor's log.

"Two weeks ago today," her father continued, skipping ahead, "Princess Nickisha was late to her math lesson by thirty minutes. Excuse: was eating lunch with her friends and forgot they were serving dessert. One week ago today, Princess Nickisha came home after curfew by fifteen minutes. Excuse: she was playing a hiding game and was the last to be found. Four days ago Princess Nickisha was late to her etiquette lesson by twenty minutes. Excuse: she had seen a frog hopping strangely and had decided to mimic it's hop."

Nicky smiled at the memory of the frog.

"Two days ago, Princess Nickisha was late to her music lesson by twenty five minutes. Excuse: she was playing Quibthrow and a squirrel ran across the court carrying her friends' necklace, so they had to stop the game and chase it. One hour ago," he said, laying the scroll down, "Princess Nickisha was late for her royal banquet fitting by one hour. Excuse: yet to be recorded." He looked meaningfully at his daughter.

"Um, she was running home when she was forced to hide from a sorcerer duel," she said.

"Was she now? And who was dueling?" the King asked.

"Kale Sefton and I think his name was Volcanis," she replied.

"That's strange, because if you had been coming home on time, you would have missed the duel by a good twenty minutes."

"I would have?" she asked, grimacing.

"Yes, you would have," he replied sternly.

Nicky exhaled, defeated.

"Nicky, you have to learn how to keep track of time. This is the sixth time this month. This month!"

"I know," she replied.

"You're fourteen now. I've told you before, work before play. It's time you start remembering that."

"I do remember," she answered, "Most of the time. It's just hard to remember that when I'm having fun."

Her father did not look convinced.

"I'm trying! I really am!" she said.

"Just, try a little harder or I might have to send someone for you to make sure you're on time."

"I'll try harder," she said quickly. No doubt he would send Aika, a cranky retired sorceress who took time *way* too seriously.

The King sighed. He seemed agitated. Nicky figured it was from the sorcerer's duel. The first duel had been a year before, between the Trune and a young sorcerer, probably an apprentice in his last years. The next one had been four months later, the opposing sorcerer about the same age as the first. After that, the duels had been closer together, although all with older apprentices. Some had challenged the King's Sorcerers, others had been younger and had just caused mischief, not all of it harmless. Nicky had once snuck into a sorcerer meeting for some answers. She discovered that many of the mysterious sorcerers were around the age of twenty five, the age most apprentices graduate. In fact, so many were the same age that the King's Sorcerers decided that someone was training the evil apprentices. Maybe all were being trained for the same purpose. They doubted it was to protect the Kingdom, the goal of the King's sorcerers. The King's sorcerers had decided to call this unknown group 'the Outlaws.' Nicky had been discovered eavesdropping and kicked out of the meeting before she could find out anything else.

Another time, just a few weeks ago, she had been with her father when one of the sorcerers had told the King that the Kale had dueled a young sorcerer and had vanished, forcing his apprentice to take over the role before officially becoming a King's sorcerer. Most had faith that the new Kale, Sefton, would do a great job, since he had the sorcerer elders, retired sorcerers, to guide and advise him. Nicky suddenly became aware that her father was standing, and jumped back to reality.

"Alright," he said, "let's go to that fitting before the fitters decide to leave."

And with that, father and daughter stood up and walked out of the room.

A Story Teller

Philo stood outside the Story Teller's workshop with eight other children around his age. Every first through fourth day of the week, their supervisor, a tall man with slowly graying hair, would take them around town, introducing them to various occupations. Today, the children were being introduced to the Story Teller.

"Alright children," their supervisor announced, clasping his hands together. "Any questions before we see the presentation?"

"I have a question," mumbled one boy. "I don't like telling stories, and I'm not very good at it either. Do I still have to be here?"

"Yes, because you might hear or learn something that completely changes your way of thinking. What if you learn that you don't like telling stories one way, the way you tell them now, and the Story Teller shows you a whole new way of storytelling?"

The child shrugged in agreement but he still looked doubtful.

With that, the supervisor opened the wooden door and the children filed into the stone building. When the supervisor closed the door behind them they were engulfed in darkness. Still used to the bright sunshine, Philo rapidly blinked his eyes until he could see again. The room had no windows. Only candles placed every few feet on the walls and floor lit the room. There were enough candles for Philo to see the basic structure of the area, but not enough to see detail. He became aware that they were in a small hallway with a doorway to the right. As the children shuffled through, Philo noticed an empty chair, its back to the middle of the far wall and candles all around it. Also sitting around it were about twelve young children. Philo heard a few children in his group groan when they saw them. He figured it was because the oldest child sitting around the chair looked about seven, while the youngest in Philo's group was thirteen. The supervisor led them to some benches near the walls, all facing the chair. As they drew closer Philo noticed people of all ages were sitting on the benches, most likely brought along for the little ones. He glanced at the children who had groaned and saw that they were looking a bit more optimistic for the story as well. Once they had all claimed comfortable positions on the benches, a door behind the chair opened. Out walked a young woman wearing a simple dark green dress with a leather belt. She had soft features and light brown hair. She sat down on the wooden chair, the young children scooting closer as she did. The Story Teller began to speak.

"A quick word before I begin," she mentioned with a gentle voice that could be heard from all corners of the room. "To the children here to learn how to be a story teller, let me give you some tips. Pay attention to how I speak, when my voice is loud or soft, happy or sad. And watch my movements as the story goes on."

She softly cleared her throat, and began.

"Close your eyes," she said, waving her arm to show an imaginary landscape. "And imagine a place with absolutely no people. No houses, no kingdoms, no roads. Just trees, and water, and land. Everything is peaceful, everything is quiet. When suddenly! A huge rock fell from the sky!" she raised her hand and stared at the invisible rock. "Now this rock was enormous! Bigger than me, bigger than a house, bigger than the Palace!"

"Was it this big?" a young child asked, stretching her arms as far apart as they could possibly go.

"Oh no, that is *way* too small. This rock was the size of our whole island!"

The younger children gasped. "No!" exclaimed several in disbelief

An older child sitting next to Philo leaned over and whispered, "I've heard this one before."

"Shhhh..." Philo shushed back, waving his hand in front of the other boys face to quite him. The Story Teller was speaking again.

"Now, this rock was falling so fast, no one could measure its speed. It was falling, and falling and--" she slammed her fist into her other hand, making everyone jump, "it hit the ground! Right in the middle of the ocean! Now when this rock hit the earth, it caused such extreme pressure that something began to form deep, deep underground. And those things were--"

"Crystals!" another young child exclaimed, standing up as he did.

The Story Teller laughed softly as she gently made the child sit back down. "Yes, it created crystals, and a brand new island! After thousands of years, a group of about fifty people who were adrift in a flotilla of boats, washed ashore on the island which, by that time had trees and animals. The men went exploring to find food. Being lost in a boat in the ocean can make you really hungry."

When they had returned, they brought back huge pieces of fruit and enormous cows and antelope. The people had never seen so much food in their lives! After they had finished their feast, their leader gathered everyone together and said, look at all the food here! This island has more food than the country we left! I say we should stay here.

Everyone agreed. So, they began building a village. That village grew and grew, until there was a whole kingdom!"

"Was it *this* kingdom?" asked a little girl.

"Yes," the Story Teller replied. "It became the kingdom of Atlantis."

"What happened next?"

"Well," the Story Teller continued, "many years later, a little boy discovered he could do things others couldn't. He could manipulate wind and stone with a flick of his wrist. One day, while he was making rocks burst into tiny bits, he felt something strange. Something in a rock nearby felt heavier than the others. He walked over and slowly, ever so slowly, broke the rock apart by holding up his fist, and gently spreading out his fingers." She demonstrated the movement as she described it. "What the boy found inside the rock was a crystal. Now the boy thought that the crystal was very beautiful with its green and violet colors, so he held on to it and went back to blowing rocks apart. Only, something was different. This time, instead of a small pop when he expanded the rocks, they now burst apart with a huge BANG!"

Every one jumped, startled by the outburst. One child screamed.

"The boy discovered that the strange crystal is what made him so much more powerful. He ran home to show everybody his new discovery. As he grew older, he was able to greatly help the kingdom advance, making houses easier to build, and holes easier to dig. Then, when he became an adult, he was made king. But he didn't stop there. He knew that there had to be others like him. So, he took his gem and went around the kingdom, having people hold it and try casting a spell. His plan worked. He found twelve other people who had been given the gift of magic. And together, they began the art of sorcery."

"Do other places have magic crystals?" asked a child.

"No," the Story Teller answered, "only here. And I'll tell you why. When that giant rock fell from the sky, something was on it. A dust of some sort. That dust was pushed into the ground so hard that the crystals picked up some of that dust, making the crystals we have here magic. And that is the story of how our kingdom of Atlantis came to be."

Silence followed. Then applause! Philo looked around at his group. The few children who had not been looking forward to listening to a story were the ones with the biggest smiles. Philo now spotted the child who had asked not to attend. He was smiling ear to ear, rapidly talking to the supervisor. Philo grinned. *There's nothing like a good story to make someone smile.*

✳✳✳

Philo was now on his way home. After visiting the Story Teller, his group had gone to see two other trades. As he and his group neared the neighborhood, Philo became aware of a large group of people. Once the supervisor had seen him safely home, Philo ran over to the crowded square. When he got there, he stood on his toes, trying to see over everyone's heads. As he stood there, tottering back and forth he fervently prayed that he would get his growth spurt by the end of the month. Finally, after getting a grand view of various hair follicles, he dropped his heels back on the ground and tapped the shoulder of the man in front of him.

"Excuse me, but what's going on?"

The man turned to him and explained. "Oh, the village overseer is collecting people to repair the damage from the most recent sorcerer's duel."

"Ah, thank you," said Philo.

"Not a problem," the man replied.

As the Village Overseer began speaking again, Philo walked over to a less crowded area so he could hear.

"Okay, just to recap," the Village Overseer became counting off items with his fingers. "We need people to repair doors, windows, walls, and roads and people to clean up everything that's been broken. We also need to begin work immediately in case those clouds over there decide to become rain clouds. Everyone please report to the craft master that you can best help. Thank you very much for your assistance!"

The Village Overseer stepped off the box he had been standing on, and the crowd dispersed, each going to the place they could be the most help. Philo was wondering where to go when he spotted his parents in the crowd. His father was a tall, thin man with dark brown hair who could turn anything into a joke. His mother was a little on the short side, with pitch black, waist long hair and beautiful brown eyes. Philo quickly ran over to them.

"Father! Mother! Wait for me!"

The couple turned and greeted their child.

"Philo!" his Father acknowledged, "How was your trade learning group?"

"Great!" he replied, "We visited the Story Teller who told us how the island came to be, a silver smith showed us how to make mirrors, spoons, and a few other things, and a decorator who showed us how to make silver and gold paint."

"Which trade did you like best?" his mother asked.

"Either story teller or silversmith. But we can talk more about that later. What are you two going to help repair from the sorcerer duel?"

"Well, I'm going to help repair the walls, and your mother is going to help clean up all the broken glass and rubble." Philo figured that much. Philo's father had helped his father in his house building business when he was a child.

Philo's father was speaking again. "What did you plan on helping with?"

"That's just it," Philo admitted, "I don't know what to help with. What do you think?"

His parents looked at him, then at each other. Finally his father spoke up. "What about repairing the windows?" he suggested, "you've helped your older brothers make glass plenty of times."

Philo hesitated. He had helped his older brothers, who were twins, with their glass making trade before. But to make glass, one needed fire. And Philo was very cautious around fire ever since the accident. He rubbed his left hand subconsciously. His mother observed the motion and sensed what he was thinking.

"Don't worry Philo; the fire will be under the control of people who know what they are doing. You won't even have to go near it."

"You're sure?" he asked, a slight hint of nervousness in his voice.

"I'm sure. Besides, your father will be right down the street if you decide to help him instead."

"Okay, I'll help with the glass," Philo answered. "Thanks for the advice!"

"Hey, take it while it's free," his father said with a shrug as a smile twitched on his lips.

"We're all going the same way, so why don't you walk with us Philo?" his mother asked.

"Sure," he agreed. With that, the family began to walk down the road.

Repairing the Village

When they got to the area where the duel had taken place, the family said goodbye and separated. Before heading over to the Glass Maker's shop Philo studied the activity. A man was handing out wooden planks with ropes attached to them for everyone to tie to their feet so they would not step on glass. After he had tied on his makeshift shoes, he realized that all the damaged doors had been taken down and put in two different piles. Doors that could be repaired were put into one, while the ones that had no hope of refurbishment were thrown in the other. Blankets were being draped over damaged areas for protection, since the repairs would take several days. People with brooms were sweeping any debris from in the houses to piles outside. Once in piles, older children would pick out large pieces of glass, wood, and clay to be put in buckets so they could be reused in the rebuilding process. Young children would then run the buckets to the appropriate trade shop, and back to be refilled.

Philo recognized a child from his side of the village running a bucket full of glass shards to the Glass Maker's shop, so he decided to follow her. When he got to the workshop he watched the girl dump the glass into a bigger bucket. After she had completed her task, she saw Philo, said hello, and ran back to collect more glass.

Philo needed to find the Glass Maker. After asking around he found him shouting instructions to various people within the workshop.

"Make sure you grind that dologem nice and fine! I don't want to see big chunks in the mixture. You! A little less limestone, I want at least *some* left for the other barrels!"

"Excuse me sir," Philo said as he approached the Glass Maker.

"What?" the man exclaimed, turning to look at Philo. He was a large man with a round, red face, undoubtedly from the shouting. As he stood there he brushed back the dark grey hair on the side of his head, since he did not have any on top.

"Hi, I'm Philo from Nom's Realm," Philo said, looking up at the tall man in front of him, "Could you direct me to someone who has more experience than I have? I've only added different minerals to the mixture."

The Glass Maker pointed over to a man of average height that had just walked in. "That man right there can help you. His name's Marlon."

Philo thanked him and, before he had even walked away, the man was shouting orders again.

Philo approached the man. "Hi, I'm Philo from Nom's Realm," he introduced himself, offering a handshake. "The Glass Maker said you have experience with glass making."

The man shook Philo's hand. "I'm Marlon Glass Mixer from Nom's Realm. Yes, I used to be his apprentice. Let me show you what to do." He led Philo to a stack of hollow stone blocks on one side of the workshop. He picked up one of the rectangular stone basin with handles on the sides. He then placed it on a long wooden table that stretched from the front of the workshop all the way to the back, and motioned Philo to do the same.

"Alright," Marlon began explaining, "This is the mold for the window. To make a window we need seven ingredients. They are preparing them for us." He walked over to a group of children grinding various rocks with mortars and pestles. Philo recognized a two of them as limestone and lake rock.

He watched as the children poured the freshly crushed powders into barrels, all set in a row. Once they had poured all the necessary ingredients into a barrel, they set it aside. Marlon picked up one of the completed barrels and walked back to the window mold. He then emptied the contents of the barrel into the mold. Philo did the same. They stirred the ingredients until they were completely mixed together, then added water and glass shards from the broken windows that were from the village. They stirred until the newly added water and glass were completely mixed in, and then placed a flat slab of stone with a metal ring fused to the top, so none of the mixture could spill out.

"What now?" Philo asked.

"Follow me," Marlon answered, picking up the stone mold by the handles placed on its sides. Philo hefted his and followed Marlon towards a door in the back of the workshop. Philo walked through the doorway and into a room with no roof and a trench stretching from one wall to the other. Two men on the left side of the room were lowering similar molds into the pit with long poles that had hooks on the ends. Two men on the other side of the room would take the molds out with the same kind of poles. As Philo drew nearer, he recognized a friend of his, magically moving the molds from one end of the trench to the other. Philo had asked him if he intended to pursue sorcery or focus on his other gifts. His friend had responded by saying that, even though he was slightly talented in sorcery, he was not interested in pursuing it, and had decided to find something he was both gifted and interested in.

Just as they reached the pit, Philo realized that it was full of wood, and that the wood was on fire. He saw people dropping shattered pieces of wood, no doubt from the doors that could not be repaired, into the pit to feed the glowing flames. Philo slowed his pace, but continued to follow Marlon, stepping slightly behind the man as he did. They handed their window molds to a man on the left side of the room, and then walked over to the right side. There, the stone molds were taken from the trench and placed into holes in a wall of ice, which was being kept cold by two other people gifted in sorcery. Marlon and Philo took two molds that had completely cooled and went back to the front of the workshop.

"Alright," Marlon instructed Philo, "take of the lid very carefully."

Philo gently took off the top of the mold, revealing smooth glass underneath. He watched as Marlon placed a rag on top of the glass. He placed his hand over the rag and flipped the mold upside-down. The window came free of the mold, revealing a grainy piece of glass. Philo did the same to his. Marlon inspected the newly made windows.

"Hmm. This window was stirred too quickly; see the lumps in the corner? Remember that for the next window you make as to not make the same mistake as the maker of this window."

They took the windows outside the workshop and set them on a blanket next to some previously made windows. There, they were reexamined and, if the window was too grainy, it was broken and reused in another mixture. Then all the good ones were placed on a cart with cloth between each window to keep them from cracking on their way back to the village. Philo helped make two more windows before returning to the village. He was amazed to see everything that had been accomplished in the time he was gone. All the windows and doors had been replaced, the cobblestone road was almost done, and the damaged walls were getting their finishing touches. He found his mother and ran over to her.

"Mother! How's it going?"

She looked up from the pile of debris she was sweeping into a pile. "Philo! It's going well. We're almost done here. How did it go at the Glass Maker's workshop?"

Philo quickly explained how everything was done.

"And you were right," he said as he finished up his story, "I didn't have to do anything with the fire."

His mother wrapped her arm around her son. "See? I told you it wouldn't be that bad. "

"Thanks again," Philo said.

"Well," she said, "I see some of your friends over there. Why don't you grab a bucket or broom and go help them clean up the area over there?"

"Alright, bye!" Philo said as he ran off.

His mother waved in return, and continued sweeping.

The Fitting

The royal banquet fitting was exactly as Nicky remembered from last year. Fitters holding up different designs in front of her, designers comparing different fabrics of vibrant colors, seamstresses sewing on seams and tassels, and apprentices running around every which way. And all Nicky did was stand on a stool with her arms outstretched like a scarecrow. With every person in the room speaking franticly, since she caused them to be an hour late in their schedule, and with everyone's voice melding together, it was nearly impossible for Nicky's mind *not* to wander. She just could not help it. Her mind was always wandering, remembering fun times she had in her past and imagining exciting events that might be in her future. She was imagining herself racing Philo up a tree when she was suddenly snapped back into reality by a sharp, "Princess Nicky, please keep your arms up! We only have so much time," from a very time conscientious fitter.

"Sorry," she muttered, straightening her arms. She briefly wondered if he was related to Aika. Just then one of the fitters who had been attending to her father came into the room.

"Introducing, King Neptus in his new royal banquet robes!"

Nicky turned away from the mirrors to see her father walking into the room. His robes were of a shimmering blue with sea green and silver tassels around the wide cuffs and down the front. On his head was his formal crown, a gold band with a sapphire placed in the front, directly over his forehead. Personally, Nicky preferred the casual crown, a simple band of green cloth with a yellow stripe going all the way around. Instantly the entire room exploded with praise from the fitters, designers, seamstresses, and especially the apprentices. Neptus looked right at Nicky and gave her a questioning look. Beaming, Nicky gave him a nod and he smiled. He knew that most of the praise from the fitters was respect, even if his robes did look good.

"So, how soon is Nicky's dress going to be finished?" Neptus asked the fitter that had just told Nicky to keep her arms up.

"About three and a half minutes, your highness," he replied.

"Very good. I'll be waiting outside." The King left the room and everyone began working twice as quickly as before, which Nicky had not thought was possible. Exactly three and half minutes later Nicky walked out of the room wearing an aqua blue dress that fell just below her knees with gold and orange tassels around the bottom and an orange and blue sash that wrapped around her waist and hung down the front. Since she had let her bangs grow out, the front portions of her hair were tied off near the ends, and on her head was a silver band. Again, she wished she could wear her favorite casual crown, blue leather with an orange stripe.

The King began clapping as Nicky gave him a twirl.

"Beautiful! Simply beautiful Nicky! An amazing job on both our outfits, as usual." He smiled at the fitters, seamstresses and designers who all bowed in return. "Glad we could be of service."

After the robe and dress had been safely stored in a closet, Nicky and her father went for a walk in one of the many gardens, like they always did when either had spare time. Nicky enjoyed this time with her father. With the royal banquet in less than a week, he had been very busy trying to organize everything. She smiled as an image of her father wearing an apron and holding a broom and to-do list popped into her head. Her smile instantly faded into a small grimace when she remembered her disapproving Aunt Frithga would be there too.

"Father?" she asked.

"Yes?" he answered.

"I was wondering, do *all* of our relatives have to come?" Her father made a sound that started off as a chuckle but ended in him clearing his throat.

"This is about your Aunt Frithga, isn't it?"

"Well, yes," she answered. "Does she have to come?"

"Of course she does. Every member of the royal family comes to the banquet. Not only is it a tradition, which you already know, but it gives every family member a chance to be informed of what's going on everywhere else. You know that too."

"I know. I just thought that, maybe, things had changed since last time I asked."

King Neptus looked at his daughter. "The last time you asked was two months ago."

"It could happen," she replied. "By the way, who's going to be playing at the banquet this year?"

Every year, the banquet started off with the entire family listening to various musicians from around the island.

"The same group as last year."

Nicky groaned inwardly. She could not stand that group. It's not that they were not talented, they were. But their music was so slow that Nicky had almost fallen asleep. Much to the disapproval of Aunt Frithga. "You do know that I almost fell asleep, right?"

"Oh yes, I did notice your head was bobbing up and down, though not to the music." Her father smiled at her.

Nicky was suddenly struck with a brilliant idea. "Could I come to the banquet after the music ends?"

Neptus considered this for a while. Finally he answered with, "Well, I don't see why not. Alright. But you absolutely have to be at the banquet the moment the music stops, okay?"

"Okay." Nicky answered, "Thanks."

As they continued on, their conversation shifted. They talked about the subjects, Quibthrow, Nicky's lessons, the latest jokes, and Neptus' new idea on how to get water to crops in the middle of the island. They had just passed by the orange and yellow poppies when Nicky asked, "Father, what have the sorcerers told you about the Oracle's prophecy?"

The king's smile faded a little. "Where did you hear about that?"

"In the sorcerer's council meeting."

"Nicky, what have I told you about eavesdropping?"

Nicky stared at her toes. "I'm sorry. I was curious."

Her father sighed. "How much did you hear?"

"Only the first line of the prophecy, that Bacillus made his move, and we have to make ours without making him suspicious."

Her father gave her a look. "And you want to know more, don't you?"

"Always."

He sighed again. When he did not continue Nicky gave him one of her best stares.

"Alright! Alright," he exclaimed, "I'll tell you this. The sorcerers haven't told me much, but they have told me that things might get a little difficult. They figure that Bacillus is sending his sorcerers after the Kale because the Oracle lives within his realm."

"Why would he want the Oracle?" Nicky asked.

"He might want to keep us from learning anything of his plot. Or he might think capturing the Oracle would give him the upper hand."

"So he is planning something," Nicky stated.

"It sure looks that way," Neptus agreed.

"Should we move the Oracle to a safer place?"

"We've thought of that." The king replied, "But since each sorcerer and sorceress have their own duties in their own realm, it could result in disaster if one of them were to suddenly have the responsibility of the Oracle along with their other duties. Besides, our young Kale is well equipped to keep the Oracle safe, despite his youth."

"I see," she replied.

Nicky thought about this for a while. "So how much of the prophecy have they told you?"

"Absolutely nothing." The king said. "Usually if they don't tell me it's because it doesn't concern the whole kingdom. But something tells me that this time they're not telling me because of fear."

Nicky considered this. Before they could say anything else, one of the kings' attendants came running up.

"Sir, the musicians need your advice on what songs to play and when."

The king sighed. "Sorry to stop the conversation, Nicky."

"It's alright. Go save the musicians," Nicky smiled.

Her father smiled back and left with the attendant. Usually it was Nicky's job to attend to such minor tasks. Things like the color of the decorations, what appetizers the cooks would serve, and what music the entertainers would play. But the King knew that Nicky did not care very much for the music that the musicians would be playing, so he took pity on her and did that particular task for her.

Nicky continued through the garden, lost in her thoughts.

She had been walking for some time before she realized where she was. Unintentionally she had veered slightly to the right and had walked out of the gardens and right into the Kale's realm. The island was divided into twelve realms, one for each of the sorcerers and sorceresses. Each realm was a rough triangular shape starting at the center of the island and spreading towards the edge. Nicky remembered the lines on the floor of the sorcerers' conference room. She figured the lines were the borders of the actual realms. Nicky stopped walking. If she continued on her current path, would be walking right into the Oracle's mysterious garden. She had never been there and rumors warned against it. But what else could she do? The sorcerers were not even telling the King anything, why would they tell her? She had to figure it out on her own. Then, without another thought, Nicky continued towards the middle of the realm, where the Oracle lived.

The Equalizers

"Reliquit, run faster! Quattuoro, your arms look like a fish out of water, stop flapping. You three! Stop talking, start running!"

It was a normal day for the nineteen year old who was yelling at the runners. Fidus, currently one the oldest apprentices of the Equalizers, was sitting in the health room supervising the younger apprentices running laps around the room. His grey eyes following their every movement. Apprentices usually received special jobs at their fifth year of apprenticeship, but Fidus had received his in his fourth year since he had mastered the element of light a year earlier than normal. He smiled as he pictured his peers just now getting their jobs. His smile faded and he groaned, leaning his head against the stone wall, as he noticed the three apprentices starting to lag behind again.

I told them to stop talking, he muttered to himself. When Fidus was in charge of the Health room, and he usually was, he never said anything twice. He would only give the inadequate apprentice one warning, and then he would cast a spell to punish them if they failed to do as he said. He contemplated what type of magic to use for the occasion. After a moment he settled on water, one of the elements he was pursuing. Keeping his hand low, he made a flicking motion with his fingers. Immediately, three fist-sized blobs of ice cold water materialized behind the slower children and slammed into their backs. With exclamations of surprise, they all put on bursts of speed, instantly forgetting whatever they were just talking about.

After a few more laps and a couple more soaking wet children, Fidus called out that they could stop. About half of the apprentices collapsed on the ground, while the others made a beeline for a drink of water.

As the young apprentices relaxed and began talking to one another, now that their laps were complete, Fidus walked over to the wooden table and began recording their times on the Health scroll. He sat down, reached for the quill pen, and then stopped. Quickly looking around to see that no one was watching, he held out his hand to ink well. He figured that since ink had a high amount of water, he may be able manipulate it. Closing his eyes, he imagined the ink lifting from its container in a small, even string and on to the paper in nice even lines. He felt a chill run from his shoulder to his outstretched hand and opened his eye a slit. The ink was doing exactly what he wanted. Just as he was beginning to write out the reports—

"How are you doing that without your staff?" exclaimed a young apprentice.

Fidus, startled by the outburst, lost concentration and the ink fell, splashing all over the table and down to the stone floor. Fidus turned on the apprentice with startling speed. The child was one of the newest apprentices, recruited only a few weeks ago. He had not yet learned to fear those of a higher rank. He had not yet learned to fear Fidus. Fidus threw his fist up into the air next to his face and flicked out his fingers, intense warmth quickly spreading from his finger tips and wrist to the middle of his palm. Immediately an intensely bright orb of light appeared before the child's face. With a cry the apprentice stepped back, flinging up his arms to shield his eyes.

"You are to never question me, or anyone of a higher rank than you, when they are casting a spell! Do not approach me when I am completing a task. This orb of light is a warning. Don't make this mistake again."

Fidus dropped his hand and the light vanished. The child blinked a few times, and then bowed.

"I-- I'm sorry. I-it won't happen again," he stuttered apologetically.

"Good," Fidus said tersely. "Now go away."

The apprentice nodded hastily and ran off. Fidus turned to look at the table. Ink was everywhere. Soaked into the scroll and the table, staining the floor, and still dripping into huge puddles. He muttered a frustrated word and began reversing the drying process in the scroll. Closing his eyes he held up both hands and imagined the ink coming out of the paper and going back into the well. The familiar chill ran from his shoulders to his hands and he opened his eyes. The ink began to rise from the paper, forming an orb before returning to the well. Fidus looked the paper over finding a few splotches remaining. He focused all his thought on the ink but most of it refused to come out. After trying a few times he stopped in frustration. He would have to explain those to the record keepers, a conversation he was not looking forward to. He next set his attention to the puddles and stains on both the floor and table. Using the same technique, he was able to get most of it out of the wood and all off the floor. He glared angrily at the now purple wood for a few seconds before finally writing down the times of the apprentice's laps, this time with a quill pen.

When he had finished, he rolled up the scroll and turned around. There, at the doorway of the Health room stood the apprentices and five masters, all staring at him. Fidus was suddenly worried they had seen him experimenting with the ink. He knew experimenting with magic was looked down upon unless one had received permission from Bacillus himself, the Master of all Masters and the leader of the Equalizers.

Fidus walked towards the doorway. Pretending none of the sorcerers there had witnessed anything, he began signing out apprentices to their masters, recording the time the masters had taken their apprentices from the health room next to the time they had left them there that morning. When the fourth sorcerer master had left with his apprentice, Fidus felt a hand on his arm. Turning around, he now faced the fifth master.

"That was quite amazing how you cleaned up all that ink," he stated.

Fidus relaxed. Everyone had begun watching after the accident. For now his experiment remained undiscovered.

"Thank you master," Fidus replied.

The master motioned to an apprentice to come with him. Fidus recognized the child as the one who had caused the ink spill.

"I wouldn't have had to clean up the ink if your apprentice hadn't startled me," Fidus added.

The master's smile vanished. He glared at his apprentice. "I see," he said slowly. "Well I'm sure you know that the same mistake will not happen again."

"I'm sure it won't," Fidus agreed. The apprentice hung his head as he followed his master down the hall. "I'm sure it won't."

The Master of all Masters

Fidus' leather sandals made barely a sound as he walked down a hall on his way to his master's chambers. Even though Fidus was often put in charge of other apprentices, he was still an apprentice himself. And like all apprentices, he had his own master who trained him in the art of sorcery. While he was walking, he came to a water clock at a fork in the tunnel. The clock was a fairly recent design, a raised tub of water with a spout near its base. The water would drip into a cylinder-shaped tub beneath it. As the water from the upper tub filled the lower tub, a pole with a disk of pumice stone on one end would float. The other end of the pole had notches carved into it. As the pole would float higher, these notches would interlock with a gear, turning it. And as the gear turned, the hands on the clock would also. Fidus marveled at the ingenuity. He also noted the time. He only had a few minutes before his training session.

He began walking slightly faster. As he made a right turn, he glanced at the upper wall. Noticing the rune, he muttered a spell, and safely walked through. There were spells put on multiple tunnels to prevent uninvited guests from walking freely through their underground realm, not that their enemies had ever found the Equalizers' headquarters. The runes were placed above cursed doorways to remind Equalizers of the spells. One rune would represent one counter spell; another would represent a different one. Fidus absentmindedly grabbed a small, circular pendent he wore around his neck with a grey whale engraved on it. Like all apprentices, he still had to memorize various spells to keep from being seriously injured by a curse placed on a doorway. The necklace he had kept him safe, to some extent. Instead of instant death from a curse, anyone who had this necklace would only be paralyzed until someone with the correct healing spell came and rescued him.

By now Fidus had reached his masters' chambers. Taking a deep breath, he said the proper spell as he placed his hand below a rune, and the wall he was facing split. He stepped through, wondering what his master had planned for him today. The moment he entered, he bowed from the waist.

"Welcome, apprentice," Bacillus said after a moment, his voice smooth and controlled.

"Thank you, Master," Fidus replied, still bowing.

Bacillus allowed Fidus to rise, then went back to what he was doing. He was sitting at his desk which was made of dark cherry wood with intricate carvings on the legs and sides. The top was bordered with diamonds and pearls.

Bacillus himself was tall, dark haired, and of average weight. Fidus could not help but stand in awe of him. Something about his master had a presence of power. Bacillus was dressed as fancy as his desk, his cloak of fine silk, enchanted to show others the various spells he knew. Yellow flashes by his sleeves meant he had mastered light, blue swirling around his arms stood for water, browns and greens quivering by his ankles represented mastery of earth, and the colors swirling and blinking across the rest of his cloak showed all the different duel magic he had mastered. Upon his head was a crown shaped like three mountains standing next to each other, each only half a hand's width high, made entirely of diamond. To add to the mountain look, pearl was inlaid on each tip, resembling snow.

This room was one of the largest of the underground Kingdom, as was only fitting for King Bacillus. Like every room, it was carved from stone. Encompassing the entire right wall was a window. But instead of looking out on a field or being made of glass, this one looked out at the seabed, and had a spell to keep the water out, the ocean's surface seventy-five feet above.

"Do you remember what I taught you last time?" Bacillus finally asked Fidus, putting down his feather pen.

Of course I do. Fidus thought. Aloud he said, "Yes, Master, I do."

"Then show me." Fidus walked over to the window, where there was more light.

Closing his eyes, he stretched out his arms, a chill running from his shoulder to his fingers as he pulled moisture from the air together. He opened his eyes to see the orb of water forming between his hands. Keeping his hands outstretched, he moved them away from each other, stretching and flattening the orb until he created an oval shield before him. He held it for a few seconds, before moving both hands to his left side. He relaxed his fingers slightly, and the shield, now on his left side also, one again became an orb. Fidus suddenly stretched out his fingers again, moving his right arm in a sweeping motion to the other side of his body. The orb stretched, following his hand. The water rapidly flew around him, now forming a ring, a few inches wide and about four and a half feet tall. The water continued to swirl around him, gaining speed all the while. Tiny droplets of water started flying everywhere, onto Fidus' hands and face. Fidus clenched his teeth, trying to regain control of every drop. The water flew from his face and hands back into the ring, which was now going incredibly fast. He spun the water a moment more, then straightened his arms, throwing his hands down and interlocking his fingers. The water joined together at the bottom, still spinning around him. Slowly he raised the platform up, moving his feet to balance on the swirling water. Below him the water grew higher, still swirling like a cyclone. Keeping the water swirling around and below him, he lowered the platform he was standing on. Fidus closed his eyes, concentrating as his feet hit the ground and the platform became fluid again. He let the water swirl around him for another second. The cyclone now stretched from the floor to the twenty foot ceiling, Fidus still inside the swirling water. Then, with one, swift movement, he spun around so he faced the window, throwing his hands forward. And hurled all the water through it, starting from the top, and unraveling the cyclone like a spool of thread. The spell over the window allowed water to go out, but not come back in. When the last drop had disappeared into the ocean, Fidus dropped his arms in exhaustion. He turned back and looked at Bacillus. His master's face held a stern expression. Fidus was not surprised. He had never seen anything but a stern expression on his King's face.

After a moment Bacillus said, "That will do. Now sit."

Fidus silently sighed with relief. He walked over to his usual chair, a simple wood frame with a dark blue pillow. Bacillus reclined on his throne, velvet upholstery with gold rings around the legs.

"Well," Bacillus remarked after finding a comfortable position upon his throne. "I suppose that will be adequate for now. You still have an immeasurably far way to go before you're even a quarter the sorcerer I was at your age. But as I said, that is fine for now."

Fidus felt his heart sink. He had not expected 'you're amazing, I'm so proud of you.' He doubted those words had ever escaped the lips of his master.

But still, he had at least hoped for an acknowledgement that he had progressed since the last training session. Fidus immediately dismissed the thought, though. For his master to say he did well would be comparing himself with Fidus and saying Fidus was better. When with the Equalizers, and Fidus assumed everywhere else, the only way to get respect was to be better than someone else.

"Let's face it, Apprentice," Bacillus continued, "of all the apprentices, you *are* one of the most powerful. I mean, most everyone else needs their staff to have half the power you possess without one." He sighed. Then, mostly to himself added, "Apprentices just aren't as powerful as they use to be."

"I know, master."

They sat in silence for a few minutes.

"Now that I look at you more closely, Apprentice, you don't look too well. I think your last spell may have been too much for you to handle right now."

Bacillus subtly pulled his sleeve down over his hand and slowly wiggled his fingers. A golden mirror began to form in Fidus' hands. The intricate scroll work of the frame took shape. Fidus saw his face rapidly appear as the reflective silver ran like liquid across the front, quickly becoming solid. When the mirror was completely formed Fidus turned it over in his hands. Little golden roses with emerald stems decorated the back and swirled out to form the scroll work that bordered the mirror. He marveled at the detail his master had created without a staff. Not even Fidus could create such fine artwork without a staff to focus his power. It required an immense amount of concentration, power, and effort. Truly Bacillus was the most powerful sorcerer to ever live. Fidus finally studied his reflection. He had always been a little pale, but he looked a bit more so, even though he felt fine.

"That last spell was definitely too much for you," Bacillus stated. "I believe we should skip the next training session."

Fidus' heart sank even lower as a feeling of dread overcame him. His training sessions were the only thing he looked forward too, the only time he could use his power to the fullest. Bacillus had instructed him to not use his power anywhere close to its full extent outside of his chambers. He never told Fidus why, and Fidus knew better than to ask. The apprentice figured the reason was so other apprentices wouldn't be jealous. After all, everyone was supposed to be equal. That's what the Equalizers strived for, equality throughout the Kingdom.

"Although," Bacillus continued, "I don't want you wasting your time sitting in bed and eating sweets. I suppose you could guard our prisoner. One of my top sorcerers, Volcanis, did the honors of capturing the Kale a few weeks ago. You see, and I'll explain it slowly for you, if we can get information from the Kale, we may figure out where the Oracle is. That way, if she decides to prophecy, we will have the advantage . Not that we don't already. Another sorcerer's apprentice who was watching him before is preparing for his graduation mission, so someone will need to take over guarding the Kale. I don't believe that will be too hard on you."

Fidus' spirits raised a little. "Thank you, Master. I will not disappoint you."

"I know. There's no way that could happen. We've taken away his staff and placed a spell on his cell that will counter any attempt to locate him or allow him to use magic. As I said, impossible for even you to fail."

Whatever spirits had risen in Fidus now came crashing down. He knew he was a failure. He could not even do what his master had asked of him without losing energy. After all, Bacillus was the most powerful sorcerer ever to live. He was right about everything.

The Oracle

Nicky had never seen the Oracle before. Some said that she was a cranky old lady that lived in a dead tree in the middle of a swamp. Others said that if you walked in uninvited she would cast a spell on you. Still others claimed that if you breathed in the fog that surrounded her wherever she went you would become her mindless slave and serve her forever. Nicky hesitated, then continued on. She knew that these were rumors started for the sole purpose to keep the subjects or anyone who might cause trouble out. But still, Nicky had never heard anything different so they were all she could believe, yet something propelled her forward. As she walked on, her surroundings began to change. She no longer felt like she was in one of the many colorful gardens that surrounded the Palace, but in a strange and dark legend. While she continued on, she noticed that the vibrant colored flowers were becoming darker in color and more and more sparse. The trees also were beginning to change. They had become closer together and had leaves so dark a green that Nicky was sure they were black. Involuntarily, Nicky's shoulders had become raised slightly and her eyes darted around quicker than usual. But what made her uneasy was not the thick trees or the grass that came up to above her ankles, or the mist that clung to the air. It was the silence. It was so quiet that it was like someone had draped a heavy blanket over the entire realm.

Why on Earth did I even come here? she asked herself. But even before she finished her thought she knew the reason.

Answers.

She walked for what seemed like hours. All the while, the trees growing closer, the mist growing thicker, the air feeling muggier. Suddenly, something wrapped around her leg. She stifled a scream as she fell. Nicky spun around and discovered a vine looped around her ankle. She quickly untangled herself and stood up. She knew it was just a vine, but it had felt like it grabbed her. She shivered, and continued on. The grass was now up to her knees. And the trees were so thick it was as if it the sky had disappeared. The air felt so dense she almost had to fight her way forward. She felt like she was deep underwater, the ocean pressing in on her.

And then she saw the clearing.

It was as if she had woken from a nightmare. The clearing went on so far she could barely see where it ended. The knee high grass suddenly became no taller than her feet. The flowers that had completely disappeared were brighter and more colorful than when she had started her journey. Tall, lushes green trees dotted here and there. And yet, she hesitated. The world outside the dense trees was so open, so inviting, it did not seem real. It was like a rainbow one would see just outside the storm clouds' reach. One that, if you walked closer, would disappear. Without realizing it she had hidden behind a tree, only her head peeking out around it. She stood there mesmerized for what felt like years. Not wanting to go a step closer, not wanting to stay where she was. And then, she heard the singing. It was like nothing she had ever experienced before. Later, she would realize it was more like she felt it than heard it. She did not understand a single word and was not even sure if there were any. It made her feel like she was lighter than air, like she could take a step and begin flying. And then, like few others before her, she slowly walked around the tree, and took her first step into the clearing.

✳✳✳

Nicky felt as if a claw that had been gripping her heart had just let go. She breathed in and felt as if she had never taken a breath until just then. The air was so sweet. The moment she had stepped into the clearing she began to laugh. She could not help it. Something about the open space after having the trees press in on her was absolute bliss. Before she knew it she was running out into the clearing with her arms stretched all the way out on either side. She stopped and began spinning around on one foot and collapsed into a bush abundant with pale pink flowers. She stared up at the sky that had never looked so blue. She fingered one of the many velvet-like petals she had landed on.

"They are soft aren't they?"

Nicky spun around with a start. Sitting on the large roots of a nearby tree sat a young woman. Nicky had never seen anyone like her. She was dressed in a simple purple dress that came down to her ankles and around her waist was a belt made of braided grass. Her hair was a delicate dark brown. But the most exotic thing about this woman was her eyes. They were aqua blue. Nicky knew, no matter what she had thought previously, that this was the Oracle.

"Hello, Nicky," the woman said.

"How do you know my name?" she asked.

You are wearing the princess's crown," the woman mused, "And the princess is named Nickisha, but most people call her Nicky."

Nicky touched the leather band around her head. "Right," Nicky replied. "What's your name?"

"My name is Dalania," the woman answered.

"You're the Oracle?"

Dalania smiled, "Yes, I'm the Oracle." Dalania stood up gracefully and held out her hand. "Come with me. I believe you want to ask me something."

"But you're so young," Nicky protested. "Everyone's heard of the Oracle, the legend has been around for far longer than you have."

"I am not the only Oracle," Dalania replied. "The gift of prophecy is handed down to the each eldest daughter in my family line. My mother was an Oracle, as was her mother, as was her mother. When my mother was born, the gift of Prophecy went into her and left my grandmother. When I was born the gift or prophecy went into me and left her. When I have a daughter, she will receive the gift."

Nicky placed her hand into the Oracle's and followed her towards loosely packed clump of large trees in the very center of the clearing.

"Whoa," Nicky breathed when they reached the trees.

They were tall with large roots sprawled above ground and dark bark. Few had leaves. Each tree had a staircase going up its trunk leading to different doors. They passed a few of the smaller trees and Nicky noticed windows in the bark, as if there were rooms inside the trees.

When they came to the tree in the very center of the cluster Dalania ascended the staircase. The stairs were smooth wood and felt cool against Nicky and Dalania's bare feet. They climbed about half way up the tree and the Oracle walked through a door right into the tree.

When Nicky stepped through the doorway and looked around. The inside was not how Nicky would have pictured it, although she had never been inside a tree before. The walls were a lighter brown than the outside bark, like someone had carved and hollowed the inside. There were four chairs around a table in the center of the room. It looked as if whoever had hollowed the tree had left the very center intact and turned it into a table. The chairs were also made of wood. Each chair had two straight legs that went all the way up to also form the back and two more legs in the front that were bent to form the seat. Grass and vines were woven around it to form a comfortable backing and seat cushion. The floor was smooth, showing off the rings of the tree. Dalania motioned towards one of the chairs and Nicky sat down. The Oracle walked back through the doorway and up the stairs, soon returning with a basket of fruit.

"Please, eat," Dalania said, gesturing for Nicky to take some fruit.

Nicky picked up a pear and bit into it, letting the juice fall down her throat. It was incredibly sweet. Dalania lightly set a grape in her mouth and chewed softly. Nicky had not realized how hungry she was until she noticed that she had finished her pear.

"I suppose you're wondering why I came here," Nicky started but was cut off by a small wave of Dalania's hand.

"Not here dear," she advised, "Not now."

She stood and walked back to the staircase, motioning Nicky to follow her. Nicky stood, grabbing an apple as she went. As Nicky began climbing the stairs again, she noticed that some of the larger branches of the tree had been carved flat and turned into balconies. She stopped in front of an open doorway softly chewing the apple. Inside was a bedroom. In the center of the room was something that looked like a really big pillow, which Nicky assumed was a bed. Made of green vines and hot pink flower petals, the mattress had a light blanket made of soft dandelion fluff. Nicky had no idea how it stayed together. Another doorway farther up was another bedroom. This one had a mattress made of oak leaves with rose petals peeking through. It also had a blanket made of bluebells. She looked around at the other trees, noticing they had similar rooms.

"What are the other trees for? Are there more bedrooms?" Nicky asked.

"Yes, they are for everyone who has ever come to the clearing," she replied in her sweet voice, "And those yet to come."

The Oracle stepped out onto a balcony. By this time Nicky had finished her apple. Nicky walked out after her, noticing smaller branches growing off the edge to form a kind of rail. Soft pillows made of different colored petals bordered the rail in groups of two or three. Dalania took Nicky's apple core and led her towards two pillows. They sat down and the Oracle placed the apple on the rail. A few seconds later, a bird swooped it up and carried it away. After Nicky had made herself comfortable on a lime green pillow, she looked up at Dalania.

"What is this place?" she asked.

"This is where I talk with people who visit me," she responded, "like you are now."

"Right," Nicky remembered. It seemed a shame to bring up a possibly horrific subject. "I need to know about a prophecy." Now it was Dalania's turn to sigh.

"I'm afraid I cannot tell you about that."

"But if *you* won't tell me who will?" Nicky exclaimed. "I mean, the sorcerers won't even tell the King! They're definitely not going to tell me! And—"

"No! No, it is not that," the Oracle cut her off. "It's not that I do not want to tell you, or that I think you are unable to handle it. I cannot tell you of any my prophecy's because I am unable."

Nicky stared at her. "Well, who said you can't tell me?"

Dalania sighed. "No one has told me to remain quiet. I cannot tell you my prophecy because I do not remember it."

Nicky opened her mouth to say something, closed it, and then opened it again. "Why not?"

"When I prophesy, I enter a sleep-like state. Some who have heard me prophesy have said that I completely transform. When I finished my prophecy,

I wake up, with no memory of what I said. It is like time stands still for me."

"But, how do people know about your prophecy if you don't remember it?" Nicky asked.

The Oracle smiled, "that I can answer. Do you see this necklace," she asked, holding up a mesmerizing blue pendent on a long chain. "This stone was given to me by the sorcerers. Whenever I prophesy, this stone records what I say. Then, every other day, three scribes come visit me. One translates the stone, the second writes down everything he says in the record book, and the third stays with me in case I begin another prophecy."

"I see," Nicky said. "Where do the scribes keep the record book?"

"I do not know," Dalania admitted.

"Oh." Nicky hung her head.

"But I do know that the scribes will be here in less than a minute."

Nicky's head shot back up. "Do you know if they will tell me?"

"Probably not," Dalania said, "but that does not mean you cannot find what you seek. Now go!"

Nicky jumped up. She hurriedly thanked Dalania, and ran to the doorway. Just as she was going down the stairs, she heard voices. She leapt into a bedroom, pressing herself against the wall. She had just closed the door when the scribes entered the balcony. They looked pretty much like every scribe Nicky had ever seen. Wearing their usual robes of dark green, the scribes were tall, had long fingers, dark eyes, and two had shoulder-length white-hair, while the third had black hair.

"Good afternoon, Dalania," one of the white-haired ones said.

"And to you, Balon," she responded, removing her necklace and handing it to him.

Balon took the necklace and turned to the darker haired scribe.

"Come, apprentice. Let us begin the translation."
He led his apprentice down the stairs, walking right
passed Nicky's hiding spot. Nicky glanced at the last
scribe and the Oracle. All they were doing was sitting
and talking. They were not talking about anything
unusual, just about the weather, the flowers, the
scribe's job, the Oracle's day, things like that. But as
Nicky eased herself onto the stairs, she heard
Dalania laugh. It was not a large laugh, just a
chuckle, maybe a giggle. But still, it made Nicky
pause. Something about her laugh was unlike her.
Nicky's impression of the Oracle was that she was
kind of unnatural, like she was not really from this
earth. But this laugh was so normal, so real, it did
not seem to fit. It made Dalania sound... human. She
glanced back at the Oracle and the scribe. Had she
imagined it? That little spark in both their eyes...
Nicky pushed the thought aside and returned to her
mission: to find the record book. Pressing her back
against the tree trunk, Nicky silently came down the
stairs. She had just reached the doorway of the room
she had first walked into when she heard voices. She
slowly looked around the corner. The two scribes
were inside. The white-haired scribe was staring at
the blue stone, murmuring something Nicky could
not quite hear. The darker haired scribe was
fervently writing down everything his craft master
said. Nicky looked closer and saw that the apprentice
was writing in the record book!

Okay, so I found it, Nicky thought to herself, *now
how do I get it?*

Just then, the scribes had finished what they
were doing, and were gathering up their writing
tools. Nicky silently jumped down the stairs and ran
to a nearby tree, hiding in the tangle of roots. She
peeked out just in time to see the scribes descend
the stairs and leave the tree. Nicky followed at a
distance. She could see the two scribes bending
down by a particularly small tree. Nicky looked
around and saw a berry bush within six feet from

where she was, and dove for it. She parted a few of the lower branches and located the scribes. She noticed a tree not too far from her current location yet closer to her destination. Mimicking a snake she had once seen, Nicky crawled on her stomach to the tree and stood up. She glanced around the tree and saw them walking briskly back to Dalania's home. She kept her back to the side of the tree opposite of the scribes, so she would not be seen.

Once they had climbed the staircase, Nicky made a beeline for the tree they had been next to. When she got there she searched for anything resembling a hiding place for a record book. She looked at the roots and dirt surrounding the tree. There. She found a root that came out of the ground slightly more than the others. Reaching her hand underneath, she began to pat the ground, her fingertips feeling for something, anything odd. Her hand closed around something long and straight. It felt smooth and cool to the touch, a metal of some sort. She felt all along the mystery object. It was a vertical cylinder, with a rounded edge on one side. On the other end was what Nicky figured was a hinge of some sort. Motivated by a sudden thought, Nicky pulled the cylinder towards her like a lever. It did not make a sound and was pulled down with ease. As Nicky let go it sprung back up, and a small part of the tree opened like a door.

Nicky reached into the tiny space and pulled out the little but thick record book. Nicky opened it up and began to read. She had no idea that there were so many prophesies. The very first entry was dated eighty years ago. Nicky stared at the date. There was no way that Dalania was over eighty years old. Was there? Come to think of it, Nicky did not know quite how old Dalania was. Was she over eighty? Nicky shook her head and focused on the task at hand. Find the prophecy the sorcerers were talking about. As she flipped farther along, she found prophesies about the kingdom, prophesies about people, even prophesied on the weather. Finally, she found it. She began to read. *Conquered by enemy that had once been friend...*

"HEY! Get away from there!"

Nicky jumped up and looked around wildly for the voice. Running right towards her were the scribes. And none of them looked happy. She hesitated, then made up her mind. Clutching the small book to her chest, Nicky turned and ran. She did not want to steal the book, but she figured that the scribes would not let her keep it. And now that they knew that she found the book, they would probably find a new hiding place. And then she would have to follow the scribes again in two days if she wanted to find it. And she had a feeling that the matter was too urgent to allow that to happen. She glanced back and saw the scribes gaining. She ran as fast as she could towards the forest.

The Prophecy

Nicky tore through the forest. Now, instead of being scary, dark and uninviting, it was perfect shelter. As the scribes' shouts grew fainter, she dashed around an unusually thick tree and stopped to catch her breath. Breathing shallowly, she listened for the scribes. For a few moments she did not hear anything, then the snapping of twigs and the pounding footsteps became audible. Judging from the sound, Nicky figured they were too close for comfort. Assuming they believed she was going back to the Palace, which she was, she ran forward a few feet, tore some branches from a nearby tree, and took a sharp left, heading to a denser part of the Kale's realm.

She had been running for a few minutes before she heard the scribes behind her again. She smiled despite herself. They had fallen for the branches she had broken. With a sudden squish, and a short cry of surprise from Nicky, her foot sank into the ground. Nicky, however, had so much momentum that she ran a few more steps before she stopped.

Great, she thought, *I've reached the marsh.* There were a few marshes on the island, but the one in the Kale's realm was the stickiest. She looked around for a moment, hoping to find something to get her out. Then she spied the rocks. There were dozens of flat rocks a few feet in front and around her. But no matter how she tried to reach them, her feet were stuck fast. She gave up on that and began studying the trees around her, until she found one with a rather thick vine right next to her. Leaning over, she stretched out her arm, lunging at the vine. She grabbed it on her second try, pulling with all her might, until her feet gave way. She easily scaled the tree, climbed to a low branch, and jumped to the nearest rock. She then used the rocks as stepping stones, and soon the marsh was behind her. Once she was safely out of the muck, she stopped to contemplate her next move. The scribes would definitely see her footprints in the mud, and probably on the rocks. And if they were observant enough, they would find them on the tree. She decided to run a few feet more to leave a path for them to discover. When her false trail had been laid, she found a large leaf, wiped off her feet, dropped it nearby, and made a sharp right, running in the direction of the Palace.

A few minutes later, she flew out of the tree canopy and into her familiar, bright garden. Barely glancing at the guard, Nicky raced up the front stairs into the Palace, just as the sun was beginning to disappear from the horizon. Once inside the doorway, she paused to catch her breath. Hands on her knees, Nicky glanced behind her just in time to see the scribe's path being blocked by the guards. She gave them a small shrug and ran to her quarters. When she was safely in her room, she shut the door and climbed onto her bed. Her bed was the latest build, a mattress raised from the floor by a wooden structure. Sprawling over her many pillows, Nicky opened the record book to the prophecy she had started to read.

Conquered by enemy that had once been friend,
the king's reign will come to an end.

His family will meet, all but one,
for she will see a quivering sun.

Much will crash without sound,
and some will fall yet hit no ground.

From this disaster will come a tale,
one handed down without a fail.

Although life will seem to disappear,
Atlantis subjects will still be here.

The city will crumble yet not decay,
if the sorcerers can find a way.

All will lie on them to mend,
assisted by enemy that is now friend.

Nicky stared at the writing. She just could not process it. The King's reign end? The subjects disappear but not really? Everything counting on the sorcerers? And then a traitor helping them? Before she could prevent it, she screamed. Clutching the book tighter than before, she burst out of her room and into the hall. She had to tell her father. She turned a corner and passed her father, going in the opposite direction at the same speed. She ran a few more paces then skidded to a stop. Her father! She spun around and realized her father had done the same.

"Nicky! What's wrong? Are you hurt? Was that you who screamed? Are you alright?"

"Hi! Everything! No. Yes. Of course not!" she replied. "I'll explain everything when we get to your quarters."

Nicky began to run again and her father followed, both a puzzled and worried expression on his face. When they reached Neptus' quarters Nicky did not even sit down before she began to read. When she had finished the King slowly lowered himself onto a pillow. Chairs were becoming more and more popular but Neptus still preferred pillows. There was silence for several seconds before the King finally spoke. "So that's what they were keeping from me."

"I can't believe they would do this to you!" Nicky nearly shouted, outraged. "I mean it says right here that you will no longer be King. And right before that it says Atlantis will be conquered! So, basically, it says you're going to be captured or you're going to..." she could not finish the thought. Her father could not *die*. Not after the sickness had taken her mother eight years before.

"I think," her father began, his voice slightly shaky. "I think it's time we speak to the Council."

✳✳✳

Neptus and Nicky stood outside the sorcerer's counsel room. The King had summoned all twelve sorcerers and their apprentices. As they walked inside, Nicky could tell that none of them had any idea why they were there. Although several of the higher-ranked sorcerers looked as though they all had a pretty good guess. The low chattering from the apprentices had immediately died down when the door had opened. The sorcerers rose from their chairs with their apprentices to their left, as was custom. Neptus looked from one grave face to the next. After he had made eye-contact with every person before him, he spoke.

"I suppose you are all wondering why I summoned you here," he began.

Nobody moved. They sensed that the matter was not a happy one from the King's voice.

"We were Sire," the Rus said at last.

"I called you here to discuss the prophecy."

There were several gasps from the apprentices as they looked up at their masters. The Trune and the Mur both cast their eyes to the floor, while the Bos's and the Rus' features hardened.

"You see," the King continued, "the Oracle has spoken. That much I knew. But what all twelve of you graduated sorcerers neglected to tell me was *what* was spoken." When no one answered, he continued. "Now, usually I trust that when you don't present me with the Oracle's prophecy, it means that it doesn't involve the whole kingdom. Something like how the paint maker should spend his money, or what crop to plant in this certain field. Today my daughter, who as you know wants to know everything and anything," the King gave Nicky a glance, "found her way to the Oracle, and asked what the prophecy was herself. She figured that, if the sorcerers wouldn't tell me, who would tell *her*?"

Rus Nevik and Nom Drach turned their gaze upon Nicky. At first glance, their eyes were cold. But as Nicky looked back she realized that there was something else there too. Guilt.

"Well, the Oracle didn't tell her the prophecy." Neptus told his audience. "But she did find this." He held out his hand and Nicky gave him the record book. The King opened the book and flipped to the prophecy they were discussing. When he found it, he looked up.

"Would any of you like to tell me the prophecy? Or do you want me to read it myself?"

Mur Alana stepped forward. Without hesitation she repeated the prophecy word for word. When she had finished she stepped back to her original place and hung her head.

"Thank you, Mur Alana," Neptus said gently. "Now that I have heard the prophecy would one of you be so kind as to tell me why you kept this from me?"

"Because the very first sentence clearly states that you are no longer going to be king," Rus Nevik stated, turning his gaze upon the King. "Would you have wanted to know that you could very well die?"

"Yes, I would," the king replied seriously.

Nevik closed his eyes and turned away. His only reason for keeping something as big as the Fall from his king and friend, had turned out to be not much of a reason at all.

"Well, now that we know about it," Nicky spoke up, "What are we going to do about it?"

The sorcerers and sorceresses looked at each other.

"We're not certain," replied Trune Sapphirell.

"But we do have a few theories," Bos Trenious put in hurriedly. "We're not completely clueless."

"Hypotheses, really," put in the Nom, Drach , ever striving to make sure all had an absolute understanding of every situation.

"Alright then, what do you have?" Neptus asked.

"Well, we know—"

"We think," interrupted Drach .

"We think," Trenious continued through slightly clenched teeth, "that when your 'family will meet' refers to the royal banquet."

The King considered this. "Anything else?"

"I'm afraid not your highness," Drach answered.

"What are you planning to do," an apprentice asked Neptus.

"Nothing tonight," the King sighed. "I'll consider what to do in the morning. As for the rest of you, do what you can to decipher the prophecy, but make sure you get some sleep. Meeting dismissed." And with that, he turned and walked out of the room with Nicky right behind him.

The Prisoner

Fidus made his way to the dungeons, a place he had never gone before. Bacillus had told him that the Kale was being kept in a cell in the very back of the dungeons. Fidus had wondered why that particular cell. His confusion must have shown on his face since Bacillus had scowled and ordered him away immediately after.

Fidus had now reached the door that led to the dungeons. There was a sorcerer sitting by the door with a record book.

"Who sent you and what is your business here?" he asked.

"King Bacillus sent me. I'm here to guard the Kale."

The man nodded and wrote down the information in the record book.

Fidus opened the door and noticed two things: One, there was a steep, narrow staircase; and two, it descended into complete darkness. He knew that the Underground Kingdom rested on the ocean floor, but what he did not know was that there were rooms below even this. He stood there for a few minutes, wondering why it was so dark, until he realized that the phosphorescent moss that grew in the chambers above did not exist down by the dungeons. He took a step down the staircase, closing the door behind him. He was instantly engulfed in absolute darkness. He stood there a moment, then held up his hand. A familiar warmth spread from his wrist and fingertips to the middle of his palm as he pulled any light from

around him and gathered it into an orb. He squinted
his eyes until they became accustom to the bright
light, then continued down the staircase. His
footsteps, usually muffled by the moss that clung to
every wall in the Underground Kingdom, echoed
loudly. He quickly slowed his pace, but kept walking.

Unlike the rough walls of the tunnels Fidus was
used to, everywhere he looked was absolutely
smooth. As he continued descending the ever
continuing staircase, he ran his left hand along the
wall. It was colder than he had expected and covered
in slime. He pulled his hand away quickly but the
cold lingered in his fingertips and spread to the rest
of his body, causing him to shiver. He began to
notice that the farther down he traveled, the colder it
grew. He could not quite tell what it was, but
something about the dungeons unnerved him. He
slowed his footsteps even more as to not break the
silence. It was now so cold that just as Fidus was
about to attempt a heat spell, something he had not
done before, the staircase leveled out.

Fidus walked down the hall for a few minutes
before he came to a fork in the road with three
different paths. A sharp left turn, a sharp right turn,
and a tunnel that went straight ahead. There was a
spell over each path, forming a magical door.
Bacillus had told Fidus that the Kale was in a cell in
the very back of the dungeons, but before he could
figure out which doorway lead to his destination, he
heard a small noise coming from the left tunnel.
Fidus quickly found the rune over the doorway,
spoke the proper incantation, and walked safely
through.

Once inside he found himself in another tight
tunnel, only instead of walls, the corridor was lined
with cell bars and doorways sealed with spells. He
walked slowly down the aisle way, glancing through
the stone bars and into each cell as he walked by it.
After passing ten empty, musty cells, he found the
Kale huddled in the farthest corner of the last one.

The King's Sorcerer was currently covering his face, shielding his eyes from the sudden light. Fidus dimmed the light enough that the prisoner could uncover his face, but Fidus could still see. Fidus studied the Kale's features.

He was in his mid-fifties with grey streaking through his dirty blond hair that stuck out so his head looked like a wilting sea urchin. His cloak, which was a perfect fit before he was captured, was now draped over his thin body. He rapidly blinked his faded blue eyes, trying to adjust them to the light.

"Who are you?" he asked. His voice was the pitch of an old man, but much stronger.

"I'm the one who asks the questions," Fidus retorted, making his voice as harsh as he could.

"Ah, alright then, ask away," the Kale responded in a more jovial tone than someone who was being kept in a cold cell should have.

The Kale's eyes, now completely accustomed to the light, surveyed the room. Fidus observed him study the stone bars of his cell. The Kale's eyes now moved over to the stone walls, stone ceilings, and stone floor. Without realizing it, Fidus was doing the same, studying the area to gather his bearings.

"You Outlaws sure like stone," the Kale muttered, mostly to himself.

"I demand to know what you mean by that!" Fidus stormed, suddenly angry.

"Well it's nothing to get upset over," the Kale replied simply, "I just stated that you seem to have a liking for stone and there's nothing wrong with that."

"That is not what I meant," Fidus growled, "I demand to know why you call us outlaws."

The Kale stared at him, calmly stating, "Isn't it obvious?"

"No, answer me!" Fidus nearly yelled.

The Kale changed the subject. "I thought you were the one who was supposed to be asking questions."

Fidus stared at the man behind bars with distaste. Here he was, a prisoner, and he *dared* question his guard? "How dare you question me!" Fidus held up his right hand, the one with the orb of light, and hurtled the glowing sphere at the Kale. As it flew through the air it grew brighter. It reached the doorway of the Kale's cell and exploded into a million sparks. The two people were now plunged into darkness.

Fidus stared through the dark. *The spell over the doorway must keep magic from going in or out of the cell,* Fidus figured. *I wonder if someone could use magic if he was already in the cell.* He held up is hand and gathered the light back into an orb, revealing his surroundings once again.

"Do you feel better now that you've thrown something against a wall?" the Kale asked calmly.

"Stop asking questions!" Fidus exclaimed, "You have no idea what you're doing!"

"Alright, I won't ask any more questions. But I have to say, and I know I'm stating the obvious here, that you, the one supposed to be asking questions, have not asked a single one."

They stared at each other for a minute, Fidus not sure what to say.

"I think," the Kale continued, slowly standing as he began pacing the cell, "that you are afraid to ask questions, am I right? Or perhaps is it that you don't even know *how* to ask one?"

They continued staring at each other, Fidus angry and the Kale calm. The Kale continued speaking.

"If I'm correct and you really have forgotten how to ask questions in your years as an apprentice here, you wouldn't be able to ask me *how* to ask a question. So I shall give you a quick lesson. Start with one of these words: Who, what, where, when, why, can, will, is, should, would, could, or how. Also, your question cannot sound like a command. Do you understand?" as the Kale finished explaining, he realized he ended with a question. "Oh! You can start a question with the word 'do' also!"

It was then that Fidus smiled. His smile had no amusement in it, for he believed the previous conversation contained very little humor. His smile was arrogant, like he just discovered how the Kale thought and had decided to use his knowledge to his advantage. Besides, Bacillus had told him to get as much information out of the prisoner as possible. Maybe there *was* a time when asking questions was not looked down upon. Maybe that time was this.

"Alright, prisoner," Fidus began with a smug tone, "I'll play your game. I'll ask you a question. Actually, I'll ask a lot of questions, one for every question starter you gave me. Let's start with w*ho* are you?"

Fidus thought he saw the Kale smile slightly, but the lighting was not at its best so he figured he had imagined it.

The Kale replied, "I am Kale Norvus."

"Your title means nothing here *Norvus*," Fidus continued. He felt strange to be asking questions again, though he felt someone would walk in at any moment and catch him red-handed. He had been an apprentice for five years and since the very beginning he had not asked a single question. He had seen what happened to those who questioned what they were told and knew he never wanted it to happen to him. Although, he *had* been told by Bacillus himself that he was to get information from the Kale, and this seemed the only way to get it. He continued with the questioning. "*What* is your duty in the kingdom of Atlantis?"

"My duty is to protect the realm under my authority, create rules which the people within my realm must follow, enforce those laws, rebuild and repair things that the people within my realm cannot rebuild or repair, and report back to the King once a month on the activities within the realm."

Fidus focused on the Kale, a cold fire in his eyes. "Is that every Palace sorcerer's duty?" Fidus asked, his tone no longer arrogant, but serious.

"Yes."

"So, if there are people in your realm, is it your job to protect them, keep them safe?"

The Kale briefly contemplated this. "Yes, I suppose keep them safe is the same as protect."

"Then why didn't the sorcerers do anything when the sickness came eight years ago?" Fidus asked. He was deadly serious now. "Why did you allow us to grow sicker and sicker, and eventually die? What were you doing that was so important that you couldn't heal anyone?" He now began to approach Norvus. "You *all* had the power to save our families," he pointed to himself, "to save *my* family! Why didn't you and the other sorcerers come to our aid when our whole village was dying? Why didn't you do anything to prevent my sister's death at birth?" Fidus' voice grew louder with every question until he was shouting. "Why didn't you save my father when he caught the sickness and died?" He had reached the bars of the cell and was gripping them with both hands, face to face with the Kale. "Your job is to repair what's broken and cannot be repaired by people within the village, right? Then why didn't you repair my mother's mind when she went crazy from grief?" He had never before asked so many questions at once, even when he was allowed to ask them. They just seemed to tumble out of his mouth on their own.

He stood there staring at the Kale, breathing hard. His knuckles had turned white from holding the cell bars so tightly, his face was inches from the Kale's. His thoughts swam with images of his family, pictures he had tried to push to the very back of his mind. It suddenly dawned on Fidus that he had just revealed a major part of his past to someone, something he had never done before. He quickly stepped away from the cell, turning his face away from Norvus and closing his eyes to hold back the emotion that threatened to come pouring out. Even though he wanted otherwise, Fidus still could never think of his family without grief welling up inside him. He forced his breathing to slow down.

The minutes crawled by in silence. Norvus finally spoke.

"I am very sorry," he said softly. "We tried our very best to develop a spell that would save those who were sick, but we were unsuccessful. We sorcerers can do many wonderful things, but when it comes to the human body..." he shook his head. "The human body is far too complex for us do more than heal cuts and bruises. Whenever we try healing something deeper, like a sickness or a fatal wound, something else always goes wrong. If the patient doesn't die from the sickness, he usually dies of something else, though we can rarely discover *what*. But don't think that we, the King's Sorcerers, didn't lose anyone close to us. Everyone lost someone. Even the queen died during those two horrible years. And *please* don't think we did nothing. We did all we could."

"Well, it wasn't enough," Fidus stated flatly. He now stared coldly at the Norvus, his sadness buried deep within himself.

Norvus sighed deeply. "I know," he nearly whispered.

A somber mood settled on the room and a long stretch of silence followed, in which the Kale sat back on the ground leaning his back against the wall. Fidus studied the cells, walls, floor, and pretty much anything in the area to keep his mind off of his past. He found patches of mold, a small water clock, and a dusty cobweb, the spider long since dead.

Finally the Kale said, "Why don't you practice your magic, since it seems we're done with the questioning."

"I can't, not here," Fidus replied, "I'm not allowed to practice magic outside the room I train in. My master forbids it." He was done acting strong. After he had told Norvus about his past, told him how weak and hurt he really was, he no longer wanted to fake being superior. "Besides, I can't perform a spell without losing a large volume of energy. And I can't guard you without energy."

"Are you joking?" Norvus asked, amazed. "The moment you walked in I could sense you had much more power than the average apprentice your age. I'd think you could perform a fair number of spells without tiring."

"Well, you're wrong, partly. I *can* perform quite a few spells, but each one drains my energy like that," he replied, snapping his fingers. But Fidus could not help feeling better about himself when Norvus said he had more power than other apprentices his age. Of course, Bacillus had told him he was powerful also, but he had meant it as a terrible fault, not something he should be proud of.

"What exactly did he forbid?" the Kale asked after a moment. Fidus glared at him. "Right," Norvus remembered, "no questions from me. Although, I am quite curious."

Fidus sighed. "I don't know what it's like up at the surface, but here in *our* kingdom we strive to create equality everywhere. I'm a little more powerful than other apprentices, so I can't expose my full power. If I did, then we apprentices would no longer be equal."

The Kale stared at him, almost dumbstruck. "Wait, let me make sure I understand." He said, no longer leaning against the wall but still sitting. "Everyone here is to be an absolute equal, right?"

Fidus sighed. There was no stopping this man from asking questions. He nodded in answer to the Kale's question.

"So that means," Norvus continued, "everyone here is to be treated with equality, no one is better than anyone else?"

"Right."

"Everyone has to *pretend* to have equal abilities? No one can be better than anyone else in *anything*?"

"Right," Fidus answered again. This was common knowledge. How did the Kale not know this?

The Kale looked at him, his mouth slightly open. He shook his head as if to clear it and began a different approach.

"Okay," he began. By the tone of his voice, Fidus could tell the Kale thought something was seriously wrong, though Fidus was not sure what.

"What is the problem with asking questions?" Norvus asked.

Fidus looked confused. "You just asked me, why asking a question is bad, by asking a question."

"Is that not common?" the Kale responded innocently, with another question.

Fidus responded with a shake of his head as he sat there and marveled at how curious Norvus was. It reminded him of a toddler that had lived in his village.

"In answer to your first question, we get punished whenever we ask any questions," Fidus responded.

"And who punishes you?" The Kale asked.

"The Masters."

"Are they allowed to ask questions?"

"No," Fidus shook his head, "the Masters of apprentices are also not allowed to ask questions."

"Well, then, who punishes them?"

"The Masters of Masters, the next rank up."

Norvus continued his order of questioning. "And what about them? Are they allowed to ask questions?

"No--" Fidus started, then cut himself off. He had seen Masters of Masters questioning people, but had never heard of them being punished. "I-- I don't know, I've never asked." Fidus saw the Kale smile slightly at that statement. "But I think they might be able to."

"Hmm." Norvus said thoughtfully. "Is there any rank above them?"

"Yes," Fidus replied, "the Master of all Masters, King Bacillus."

"And can *he* ask questions?" His tone made Fidus feel as if the Kale already knew the answer.

"Yes, and before you ask if there's any rank above him, there's not. He's the very top."

"And he makes the rules?"

"Of course he does, he's the king."

"What a lie!" the Kale exclaimed, pushing himself off the ground with such force that he nearly fell over instead of standing up.

"What did you say?" Fidus did not know whether to be offended or angry. After all, the Kale was a prisoner, he had not lived in the Underground Kingdom, he did not know their way of life.

"What a lie!" the Kale repeated, now firmly on his feet. "Your 'king' makes the rules, but doesn't have to follow them? How can you expect him to have your best interest in mind?"

"King Bacillus is a brilliant man and the most powerful sorcerer and master to ever live, how dare you question his reign!"

The Kale stared at Fidus with serious eyes. "If authority is not questioned, they will abuse their power any way possible. Not because they're evil, but because it's human nature."

Fidus was about to respond when he glanced at the water clock at the end of the room. It was four o'clock, the time Bacillus had told him he could stop guarding the Kale.

"This conversation is over," Fidus stated. He stood and stalked out of the dungeons.

Fidus was furious by the time he had returned to the Underground Kingdom. The Kale had wormed his way into Fidus' past and questioned everything Fidus had ever stood for, something he had no right to do.

But in the very back of Fidus' mind, buried so deep he did not even know it was there, a seed of doubt had sprouted.

Unraveling Riddles

"How about we cancel the banquet," Nicky suggested the next morning at breakfast, "that way the family won't meet together."

"Nicky," Neptus sighed, "by the time the message would reach our distant relatives, they would already be on their way over here."

Nicky considered this. "What if only some of our family came? Then, we could have part of the family meet one day, and the other part come some other day. That way our entire family wouldn't be here at once. How about that?"

"Most of our family is already here," Neptus stated, "and the prophecy never says the entire family has to meet."

"But it says 'his family will meet, all but one.' Doesn't that mean *all* except for one person? Maybe we can keep two people away!"

Her father was silent.

"Well we can't just do nothing!" Nicky exclaimed, jumping up with such force that her pomegranate juice spilled and flooded the eggs on her plate. After a servant had gotten everything cleaned up and Nicky some new breakfast, her father spoke.

"Nicky, you need to stop yelling when you're angry, especially at me," he stated sternly. Then, as she apologized with downcast eyes, his expression softened, "I know you're scared, everyone is."

"Even you?" Nicky asked, returning her eyes to her father.

Neptus averted his gaze a moment, then looked straight into Nicky's eyes. "I am."

Nicky had not expected that answer. "*You're* scared?" she asked, now terrified.

"Nicky, it would be foolish not to be. The prophecy hints that the entire kingdom will crumble and possibly even die. Although, I'm more apprehensive of the course of action we are to take, and if we accidently prevent the prophecy."

Nicky's eyes darted back and forth in confusion, "Wouldn't it be *good* if the prophecy never came true?"

The King smiled softly, took a breath, and began a story, "When I was around twelve, I heard a story of a prophecy about a gardener. The prophecy said that if the gardener wasn't careful, his business would plummet. Now the gardener was so scared for his business that he began saving twice as much of his income. Now, saving that much money isn't a bad thing, mind you, people should save part of their income. Because of his extra savings, he was able to purchase newer, better equipment for his business, allowing him to work more quickly, and therefore, accept more jobs."

"So, his business *didn't* fail?" asked Nicky as her father took a sip of kiwi juice.

The king shook his head as he swallowed. "Not at that time, no. But an unexpected consequence of cutting back was they were forced to also cut back on their lifestyle. Now instead of buying things, they had to do without or make it themselves, growing their own, not as many toys for the children, that sort of thing. Now you see, the oldest son, the one who would inherit the business, didn't like the sudden switch to a poorer way of living. So when he was put in charge of some of his father's business, he was irresponsible with the saved money, and spent more than he made, causing the business to fail, and forcing the father to sell it."

Now Nicky was silent.

"You see," Neptus continued, "prophecies have a way of coming true, sometimes in the way you thought, sometimes in ways never expected. But what happens more often than not, people try to take matters into their own hands, and make it happen in a way they never prepared for, like forcing it onto the next generation."

When the meal was finished Nicky looked up at her father. "Could I at least try to figure out what the prophecy means?"

"Yes," her father answered, "just don't tell the citizens about it quite yet. I'm pretty sure that most would become hysterical."

"Of course," Nicky replied.

Just as she was leaving the room her father called out, "just a minute young lady. You *did* steal that book. Before you start trying to interpret the prophecy I want you to return the book to the scribes and apologize."

"Yes Father."

"And you need to report back here to your tutor at one o'clock for the lessons you skipped yesterday."

"Yes, Father."

With that, Nicky ran to her room to get the record book, contemplating what she would say to the scribes.

***

Nicky sat cross-legged on a hill, reading and re-reading the prophecy. Before she had returned the book to the scribes she had written the prophecy on a blank scroll. She remembered the conversation with the scribes and shivered. If she had been anyone else besides the princess, she would probably have gotten much harsher words than, 'Thank you, Princess, for returning our record book."

Of course, ever curious, she had asked why the scribes did not keep the record book with them at all times. The response had been simple. If someone with the wrong intentions were to get their hands on the book, the results could be disastrous. No one went to the Oracles forest, so it was safe there. Nicky figured that they would probably hide it somewhere else now that she had been there. Just before she had left, she had dared to ask if they could explain the prophecy of the fall to her. They had replied with a short, harsh, no.

Nicky went back to reading the prophecy. She re-read the third sentence. *"Much will crash without sound, and some will fall yet hit no ground."* Nicky stared at the words. "What does that even mean? Does everyone go deaf and when they trip, people catch them?" She sighed. There was no way that's what it meant.

"Hey Nicky."

She jumped and turned around. Coming up the hill was her friend she'd known since she was five.

"Hey Philo," she responded, rolling up the scroll and setting it on her lap.

"So, what've you been up to?" he asked plopping down on the grass in front of her. "I haven't seen you since the game yesterday. Where've you been?"

"Oh, around," she said causally, keeping a firm hold on the prophecy scroll.

Philo did not look satisfied with the answer, so he decided to take a different route.

"What's that?" he motioned to the scroll.

"It's—" she was about to say 'nothing important' but realized that wasn't quite true.

"It's..." he prompted.

"It's just a scroll full of sayings. Kind of like riddles," she finished. This was the wrong answer.

"Great, I love riddles! Can I read one?" he asked, reaching for the scroll.

"No!" she exclaimed, jerking it away from his outstretched hand. Then, noticing the strange look on Philo's face, she added "It's just that, I like being the only one who knows the answer."

"Uh, huh," he said slowly. "Then why don't you read me one?"

"Uh, no, not right now," Nicky stated briskly. "I've been reading them for quite some time now, and am getting tired of them. Why don't we talk about something else?" She figured the conversation was getting a bit dangerous. It was not that she did not trust Philo, it was just that she did not think he absolutely *had* to know about a possible end of all Atlantis life.

"O-k-a-y," Philo said a bit uncertainly. "What do you want to talk about?"

"Um, the wind? Yes, the wind. It's nice and quiet today, isn't it?"

"I guess."

"And the flowers! Look at them, all over this hill alone. And such vibrant colors."

"Nicky?"

"And the sky, look how blue it is! It reminds me of the shallows of the ocean!"

"Nicky?" Philo said a little more forcefully.

"Or we could talk about the strange way ants crawl! Just look at that one, there on the rock!"

"Nicky!"

"Hm?"

"You're talking really fast."

"So?" Nicky asked.

"Nicky, I know you! You only talk fast when you're scared," Philo stared at her. "What's going on?"

Nicky shifted uncomfortably under Philo's steady gaze. "I-- I can't tell you," she answered, lowering her head.

There was silence for a while, broken only by the breeze. Nicky gazed out at the rolling green hills. Under different circumstances, she probably would have run off and rolled down the grassy slopes for hours on end. She sighed as she looked around once more. If she had to choose, her favorite realm was this one, the Trunes'. Philo finally broke the silence.

"How high is the level of secrecy?"

Nicky smiled despite herself. Like her, Philo was always curious. "So high that the sorcerers didn't even want to tell father when they found out."

Philo was at a loss for words for a moment. "Is that legal?"

"I don't think so," Nicky responded, "If it involves the whole kingdom they need to tell him. They've never *not* told him anything this important before."

Philo whistled. "Sounds like something my uncle would do, he was very secretive when he was younger. Still is actually."

"Oh yeah, I remember him. Your uncle Berum was a farmer right?"

"No," Philo shook his head, "Uncle Tret was the farmer. I'm talking about Uncle Berum from the other side of the family. He was a scribe. He retired about a month ago."

Nicky gave a start. "A scribe?" She instantly thought of the scribes from the Oracles forest. Maybe he could help decode the prophecy.

"Yeah, that's right."

"What did he usually write?"

Philo furrowed his brow in concentration. "Um, I think he said once that he wrote labels for farmers. Like corn and stuff." He smiled and said, almost to himself, "I wonder if he ever gave Uncle Tret a discount."

Nicky sighed. Not the type of scribe she was looking for. *Well, wouldn't hurt to ask him if he knows anyone who could help me.* "Could I talk to him?" she asked out loud.

"Uncle Tret?"

"No, Uncle Berum. Where is he?"

"Probably at his house. He hardly ever leaves nowadays."

Nicky was suddenly curious. "Why? Is he ill?"

"No, he's not sick, he just doesn't like getting into conversation with people he doesn't know real well."

Before Nicky could ask why, Philo answered.

"He doesn't like the look people give him when he says he wrote labels for a lifetime, since a man's trade almost always comes up in a conversation with someone unfamiliar."

"Oh," Nicky said, satisfied. "Can I still see him?"

"Sure. Why do you want to see him though?" Philo asked.

"Oh, there's just a question I would like to ask a scribe who doesn't work directly for my father." When Nicky had returned the record book to the scribes, she had asked them if they knew what any part meant. None of them did. So she wondered if someone who had never seen the prophecy before would have a different view on it.

"Okay then, let's go," Philo responded with just a hint of a strange look. He jumped up and Nicky followed, snatching up the scroll and holding it close. Philo noticed the way she held the scroll. He figured it must be really important, more than Nicky had made it sound. Of course, that only made him want to know what was written in it even more. He hoped to find out soon.

The Raven

Philo was walking with Nicky down a small dirt trail
when he saw it. At least, he thought he saw it. A
dark shape, much like a man crouching behind a
rock a few feet down the path. When they reached
the rock, Philo jumped over it, without finding
anyone on the other side.

Figures, Philo thought. He was always jumpy
when he was around Nicky. He hopped off the rock
and back onto the path. As he looked around a warm
breeze ruffled his copper hair. Green hills, wild
lupine, poppies, and daises, the list could go on
forever, every sight more beautiful than the last. And
then he turned to Nicky. Her blond hair, her tanned
shoulders, her dark blue eyes. Especially her eyes.
The way they sparkled in the sun, or when she saw a
special flower, or when her lips curved into a small
smile when she thought of something funny. He also
noticed the way she would suddenly stoop down to
get a better look at something that had caught her
eye, whether an ant carrying something, or an oddly
colored stone, or a flower.

Just at that moment, Philo became aware of an
irritating itch in his left hand. Trying to act casual,
he looked around, going through his mental check-
list.

Okay, snakes on the path? He studied the path
both in front and behind him. *No snakes. Storm?* He
looked up at the vibrant, blue sky. *No storms for
miles. Any-*

"Philo look at this!" Nicky suddenly whispered excitedly, unintentionally interrupting Philo's thoughts. She was kneeling on the ground, slowly reaching for something with both hands. Curious, Philo lowered himself next to Nicky. There, a few inches from Nicky's steady hands, was a baby bird.

"It's a Common Brown Dove chick," Nicky murmured, "Its nest must be in that tree over there."

Philo did not question how Nicky knew what bird the chick was. She had a vast knowledge of seemingly useless facts. Like a frog cannot swallow without closing its eyes, what to do if the volcano exploded, even though the only volcano was on the other side of the island and far from the villages, and what a Common Brown Dove chick looked like.

Slowly, tentatively, she inched her hands closer to the bird, freezing when it looked at her. Then, when her hands were virtually touching it, she gently picked it up. The bird fluttered nervously as Nicky walked to the tree. The tree, really more of a sapling, only came up to Nicky's shoulders. Philo, who had followed Nicky, saw her scan the branches, until she spotted the nest. After she had softly placed the bird back in its nest, she turned and smiled at Philo. He began to smile back, but before he could, his left hand began to itch again, way worse than before. With a slight grimace, Philo clutched his hand, and looked around wildly. There, to his left, was a dark shape rapidly flying towards them. It did not look friendly. Philo darted to where Nicky was standing, rapidly waving his arms and pointing towards the thing coming at them. Nicky saw it and ran. Philo soon caught up, and both put on a burst of speed.

"What exactly is that thing we're running from?" Nicky asked Philo, slightly concerned.

"I'm not sure," he replied, "I think it's--"

Before he could finish, a huge shadow passed over them and a raven taller than Philo landed in front of the friends, forcing them to stop in their tracks.

The enormous raven stared at them, cocking its head to look at Philo, then Nicky. It stared at Nicky for a few moments longer than Philo. What happened next happened very quickly. The bird looked like it recognized Nicky, Philo's hand suddenly itched so bad it burned, and the bird lunged for Nicky. A split-second before it grabbed her, Philo grabbed Nicky's arm, pulling her with him as he dove to the ground. The raven's claws closed less than an inch from Nicky's shoulders. Missing the first time, the bird climbed into the sky, and circled around for another chance.

"Go go go!" Philo yelled, pushing Nicky off the path and onto the grass, "Don't let it get you! Head for those trees, and stay under cover. I'm right behind you."

Nicky did as she was told, running for the trees that bordered the Trune's realm, with Philo right behind her. The wind had suddenly picked up, blowing stray leaves through the air.

Oh no, Philo suddenly realized, skidding to a stop. The wind was blowing in the direction they were going, giving the huge bird an advantage. Philo looked up at the bird and his suspicions were confirmed. It was riding the wind closer and closer to Nicky at an alarming speed.

"Nicky!" Philo yelled, "The wind!"

Nicky, who had gotten quite a few feet in front of Philo, turned just in time. Seeing the bird and feeling the wind, she immediately turned on her heal and ran towards Philo, ducking as she missed the bird by a hair's width for a second time.

The two friends were now running against the wind, which had gotten very fierce. They were about to reach the other side of the hill, when suddenly, a wall of wind going faster than Philo had ever seen, blew right in front of them. With a short exclamation Philo and Nicky skidded to a stop. Philo spun around hoping to run in a different direction when the same thing happened, the wind, which had collected quite an amount of debris, blocked their way.

"Uh, Philo?" Nicky said with alarm, rapidly tapping Philo's shoulder. "We're trapped."

He turned to see where she was pointing. The wind had died down around them, but outside the walls of wind, which had now completely encircled them, it was still just as fierce. Philo thought back to a day that a hurricane had hit the island. Thankfully he had been nowhere near it, but those who had been said that the very middle was absolutely calm. Philo figured that their current situation was very much like the middle of a hurricane.

Nicky was tapping his shoulder again. This time she was pointing to the sky, where the huge raven was circling above them.

"What does it want?" Nicky wondered, mostly to herself. Philo smiled despite the situation when he heard more annoyance than fear in her voice.

The raven circled a few more times, and began to descend. Philo stood protectively in front of Nicky as the bird landed heavily on the ground about ten feet away, near the edge of the wind storm. As the bird straightened from the impact, it began to change. Its wings started shrinking, and its feathers on its body began to grow, while the feathers on its wings and face began to shrink into his skin. Nicky peeked around Philo's shoulder. There, where a six-foot bird had once stood, was a tall man with black, oily hair in a dark cloak. In his hand was a dark staff with a glowing red gem near the top, along with three black feathers. The only things that had not drastically changed were his nose, which still greatly resembled a beak, and his eyes. His yellow eyes darted back and forth between Philo and Nicky for a moment before he spoke.

"Well," he began, his voice sharp in Philo's ears, "It seems to me that you're trapped, unless you wish to blow away." He smiled at his own joke.

"Who are you?" Nicky demanded, trying to keep her hair out of her face, "and what do you want?"

"Oh do pardon my manners," said the young man, making a low, mock bow, "My name is Corvus," he looked up, "and what I want is you."

"Well, sorry, I'm not for sale," she replied.

"Oh, what a relief," Corvus laughed harshly, "It will be so much more fun to steal you."

He waved his hand, and the circle of wind that surrounded them, began to shrink as his gem began to glow more brightly.

Of course, Philo knew that he could not let Corvus take Nicky. *But how do I protect her?* He asked himself, *I can't duel Corvus. Even if I knew any spells, his cloak tells me he's mastered three spells.* He decided to risk the wind, but before he could jump through the wall, a huge tree was uprooted and flew right in front of him. Hot pain shot through his hand and he jumped back just in time. He watched the tree as it continued flying around them. It was so fast that the odds of timing a jump well were very small.

Okay, that's not going to work.

He tried to remember everything he had been taught about sorcerers, good and bad. The wind continued to close in around them forcing them to step closer to Corvus, the roaring wind getting louder every second. He looked back at Nicky, finding she had covered her ears. He racked his brain, searching for the answer he knew he had. Then, quicker than the wind that was nearly upon them, he had it.

"Hey, Corvus!" Philo yelled, the wind nearly snatching his voice away, "What exactly do you want with the Princess?"

A look of confusion crept upon Corvus' face. With a wave of his hand, the wind slowed a little, and the circle widened, though only slightly.

"What?" he yelled back.

Philo cupped his hands around his mouth. "I said, what exactly do you want with the Princess?"

Again, Corvus looked confused. He waved his hand again and the circle widened once more.

"Did you just say, 'what egg tactics do you use for the prince's?'"

Philo rolled his eyes.

"He said, 'what do you want with me?'" Nicky yelled over Philo's shoulder.

"Oh," Corvus replied, no longer confused. "Well, my master said you would probably ask that. We want her because she is next in line for the throne. And because--" he suddenly stopped as the wind around them slowed considerably. He waved his hand but nothing happened. He waved it again, then his staff. Same result.

"What's going on?" Nicky shouted, trying to be heard over the wind.

Philo looked around, rubbing the ear Nicky had yelled in. Nicky smiled apologetically and he smiled back. "I believe help has just arrived."

✱✱✱

Philo grinned. His plan had worked. While Corvus franticly tried to regain control of his windstorm, Trune Sapphirell walked through the wall of wind, the gem in her staff glowing. She was of slight build, with bushy brown hair, and soft black eyes. Her staff was made of a polished walnut wood, with the orange gem embedded in a knot near the top. She took a moment to study the situation.

"Well, Corvus," she stated, turning towards the apprentice, "I see you are causing trouble again."

Corvus looked up like he had just noticed the Trune. With a slight gasp he took a step back, releasing his hold on the wind altogether. It spun around them for a few seconds more, then stopped. The gem in the Trune's staff ceased glowing.

Now Corvus looked angry, "How dare you fiddle with my spell!"

Sapphirell ignored his statement. "I see you still insist on wasting your Creator given gifts. What were you planning to do with the Princess and her friend?" He glared at the trio. "I can do whatever I want with my gifts," he sneered.

Sapphirell sighed. "You do not understand. Now answer my question."

When Corvus refused, Nicky stated, "He was planning to kidnap me."

The Trune looked slightly startled. She turned and studied Corvus.

There were a few moments of silence. Finally she said, "Was this your graduation mission?"

"This *is* my graduation mission, not *was*," Corvus growled, "It has not failed yet."

"So, you are saying that I, a graduated sorceress, who has mastered five spells, cannot stop your mission from succeeding?"

Corvus and Sapphirell stared at each other. Then Corvus lunged, transforming into a raven in mid leap. The Trune thrust her staff forward, and a ribbon of yellow light exploded from the gem. The ribbon wrapped around Corvus, up, down, left and right until he was trapped inside a giant cage. Philo grinned when he realized it was a bird cage. Corvus began flapping his wings while squawking angrily.

"You can sit down," Trune Sapphirell informed the raven as the bottom of the cage became more solid.

Corvus squawked a few more times before finally giving up and transforming back into his human form. He sat with his legs and arms crossed, muttering under his breath.

Sapphirell turned to Philo and Nicky, her cloak shimmering with the spells she had mastered. Philo watched in awe as the different colors swirled around. The Trune was a master of light and wind, which explained why she could counter Corvus' wind storm and trap him with light. She had also mastered quite a lot of combat magic.

"What are you going to do with him?" Philo asked her.

She sighed and glanced at the apprentice, who was still pouting. "We will most likely question him on various subjects, and if he is found guilty of any crimes, contain him in a more suitable cage."

"And, us?" Nicky spoke up.

The Trune gave a small smile, barely showing her dimples. "I shall take you both to the Palace."

A Family Member

Philo had never ridden a beam of light before. The Trune had created a solid square of golden light, which Philo and Nicky had stepped on.

"It's so warm," Nicky said smiling. Philo slipped off his sandal and pressed his toes against the light. He smiled as the warmth spread through his foot and into his leg. He slipped off his other sandal.

The Trune then wove glowing walls around the border of the square to form a wall so none of her passengers would fall off. It then rose into the sky, towards the Palace. The view was amazing. Clouds whizzing around them, green hills rapidly flying by below. Philo even glimpsed part of the village in the Nom's realm off to the right through the clouds. He gripped the edge as he leaned over to get a better look at everything.

"Alright, what was your plan?" Nicky suddenly asked, turning to look at Philo.

"What do you mean?" he replied, a small, quirky smile on his lips.

"Come on Philo! As soon as Trune Sapphirell walked up you had that 'Yes! My plan worked!' look on your face. What was your plan?"

Philo chuckled. In the same way he could tell what Nicky was feeling, she could tell what he was thinking.

She was still looking at him expectantly.

"My plan was to stall Corvus long enough to attract the Trune's attention. I knew that the sorcerers have spells placed on their realms to alert

them if anything unusual happens. I just had to
keep Corvus busy until Trune Sapphirell showed
up."

"Wow," Nicky marveled. "That is so simple it's
brilliant."

Philo shrugged. "Anyone else would have done it."

"Well, I'm still glad you were there," Nicky said.

She had no idea how happy that one sentence
made Philo.

✳✳✳

They landed just outside the Palace walls. When
the square touched the grass it quickly faded, and
disappeared. The Trune now moved her hand in a
circle, as if she was washing a window with a cloth,
and a grey and purple swirling circle appeared in the
air. The middle quickly became clear and the image
of her apprentice appeared. The girl looked up and
smiled.

"Hello, Master Sapphirell! What do you need?"
she asked.

"Greetings, apprentice Lanasha. Would you
please alert five other sorcerers that I have a
prisoner?"

The apprentice looked startled. Philo did not
blame her. The sorcerers only took prisoners in a
time of war, when they were protecting the island.

"Right away," the girl answered.

The Trune waved her hand and the grey and
purple circle disappeared. Within three minutes five
purple rectangles suddenly appeared before them, a
sorcerer walking out of each.

"You may leave now Princess," the Trune said
kindly, "I believe you are needed within the Palace."

"Thank you, Trune Sapphirell," Nicky replied. She
and Philo turned and ran to the Palace gate. As they
walked through Philo noticed a group of people
walking into the Palace.

"Hey Nicky, who are they?" he asked motioning to the group.

Nicky turned to look and a huge smile broke out over her face. "My exploring group!" she exclaimed.

She took off after the eight people waving for Philo to follow. They ran up the stairs and into a hallway, dodging servants who were running around to perform various tasks. As they were running, Philo noticed eight people carrying large trunks. He slowed down a little. As he looked closer he noticed that the trunks were not from Atlantis, but from the far North.

"Hey Nicky! Are you expecting anyone from the North to come for a visit?"

"The North?" Nicky repeated, not slowing down. She turned a corner and ran straight into a woman Philo had only seen once. Philo cringed as both Nicky and the woman fell to the ground.

"Sorry!" Nicky exclaimed, helping the woman back to her feet. "I'm sorry, I didn't mean to--" Nicky stopped, stared, and groaned.

"Nickisha! You must learn how to watch where you are going!" the woman exclaimed disapprovingly with a thick Gaelic accent.

"I'm sorry, Aunt Frithga," Nicky apologized.

"Honestly," Frithga muttered to herself, pushing herself up in a standing position.

Philo also stared at the thin faced woman. She was even stranger than he remembered.

Her black hair that reached her lower back was braided with gold string. Her jacket was made from grey wolf fur, and her floor-length skirt was made of red fox fur. As she stood there, she rolled up her sleeves, which reached her wrists, revealing another shirt made from white hare fur and three bracelets made of pure gold. Around her neck were eight gold chains, the shortest nearly choking her, the longest almost the length of her torso. Philo faintly heard her soft fur boots tapping impatiently on the marble floor. Two Atlantian servants stood by her, fanning

her face with palm branches. Frithga was wearing so
much fur that Philo figured, if the two servants were
not there, she would have fainted from the heat.

"For the love of the Maker, look at you!" Frithga
exclaimed, motioning to Nicky's dress, "You are a
disgrace!"

Nicky looked down at her blue green cotton dress.
It reached just to below her knees, and her sleeves
were really just shoulder straps.

Frithga was speaking again. "Your arms are bare,
your legs and neck are exposed, you don't have an
ounce of gold anywhere on you, you have no shoes, I
wonder if you even own a pair, your only symbol of
wealth is your brightly colored dress, if it can even be
called that, you should be ashamed!"

Nicky grimaced at every harsh word.

"Excuse me," Philo spoke up.

"And you!" Frithga turned to Philo, "Your clothes
have no bright colors. You have no shoes. You're
obviously a peasant. Nickisha, why in the name of
the earth are you in the company of a *peasant*?"

"I'm terribly sorry." Philo declared loudly before
Nicky could speak, "the Princess is expected to
attend a royal meeting and I'm escorting her. Good
day to you!"

Philo grabbed Nicky's arms and quickly pushed
her around Frithga, who was announcing all the
ways Nicky resembled a peasant more than a
princess, when they turned a corner and both began
running once again.

Once they were far enough away, they slowed
their pace. Philo looked over at Nicky. She was
walking confidently as if nothing had happened, but
her face was turned away from him.

"Hey," he said softly, "are you alright?"

"What? Oh. Yes, I'll be fine." Her voice was level
but cracked slightly as she finished talking. She
moved her hand as if to brush a stand of hair out of
her face, but Philo knew she was wiping away a tear.

He placed his hand on her shoulder and they stopped walking.

"I know she hurt you," he said gently, "But you don't have to hide sadness or anger when you're with me."

She turned slowly and looked at him. He stared back with kindness and understanding in his green eyes. She sighed shakily and hung her head, a silent tear gliding down each cheek. She lowered herself to the floor, leaning against the wall. Philo sat next to her, his hand no longer on her shoulder.

"I know I shouldn't take it personally," Nicky said, wiping away her tears.

"But you do," Philo stated, "and that's okay."

They sat there for a few minutes as Nicky calmed herself down. Nicky had the ability to appear calm in most circumstances, but in reality she had to struggle to control her emotions. After a couple minutes she had composed herself enough to speak.

"I understand why she said those things," Nicky began. "Our cultures are very different. She's from a place where wealth is shown by how many wolf skins or how much gold jewelry you wear. I'm from a place where wealth is shown mostly on making lives better. Most the decorations in the Palace are gifts from people who live in the village or family from overseas. All I have to show that I'm a princess is this orange and blue leather strap around my head. It's not even worthy of being called a crown in her opinion."

"I guess she has a hard time realizing that people can be so different," Philo determined. "But have you noticed that people who know the least about something have the most to say about it?"

A small smile appeared on Nicky's face. "That's very true. So I guess I really shouldn't take what they say as truth, since they really don't know what they're talking about."

"I believe you're right," Philo replied. Then in a softer voice he added, "Do you feel better now?"

Nicky smiled. "Yes. Thank you, Philo."

"You're welcome. Now, let's go find the exploration group you were talking about." He was aching to see where they had been exploring.

They helped each other to their feet, and ran towards the meeting room.

They arrived just in time. The exploration group had all gone to freshen up and had entered the room a moment after Philo and Nicky. They greeted the princess and everyone sat down. The sorceress Quen Anrym walked into the room and the meeting began.

"Three weeks ago today," Quen Anrym began, "Princess Nickisha was placed in command of the exploration of the Quen realm. Princess Nickisha, please tell us what you hoped to accomplish on this exploration."

"Right," Nicky stood and addressed the exploration group. "On exploration I wanted to find out if crops could grow in the Quen's realm without use of magic, what the terrain is like, what kinds of animals live within the realm, and anything that is unusual or different from the other realms. Erius?" She motioned to the group leader and sat down.

Erius stood and replied, "Yes, and I'm sure you will be pleased to know that we discovered the answer to all those questions. In answer to your first question, no. We found that crops do not grow well anywhere in the realm without the use of magic. The terrain is mostly swamps. We noticed signs of four different bird species and a large cat, all of which we have seen before. There were very few insects which surprised us at first, given all the swamps, but then we discovered what was unusual about the Quen's realm. At the very edge of the realm near the ocean but still under the swamp trees, we realized that the ground was very hot and covered in salt. We performed some tests and we think the King's theory has been proved correct. That is our report, Princess." Erius sat down and Nicky stood up.

Philo looked over at Nicky and found she was barely containing her excitement.

"Thank you for your report. It's great news that what we thought about the Quen's realm is true! Please give Quen Anrym a full, written report." Nicky motioned the Quen and sat down.

"Thank you all for attending. Meeting dismissed."

With that everyone got up, and left the room.

Once outside Philo turned to Nicky. "What did they mean 'the King's theory has been proved correct?' What's your father's theory?"

"Nicky excitedly began explaining. "Well, the Gar told us that he noticed a river of lava flowed from the volcano in his realm right into the Quen's. But when we look in the Quen's realm, we couldn't find it. So, Father thought that maybe it flowed underground! The way that area of the Quen's realm is set up is, when the tide goes out, some of the ocean water is trapped inland. The underground lava then heats the water, which then evaporates, leaving the salt behind. The evaporated water then gets trapped under the dense trees, causing the thick fog that hangs around the area. Isn't that great?"

Philo stared at Nicky. He held up his index finger and opened his mouth, as if a brilliant idea had just come into his mind, then closed it as a look of confusion appeared on his face.

Nicky started again. "You know how we collect water when it rains, for drinking water?" she prompted him.

Realization immediately dawned on Philo. "Oh! I get it! We could collect the water as it evaporates and, since the lava is working all the time, not just when the sun's up, we can collect even more with less effort! That's a brilliant idea."

Nicky smiled. "And, since the theory is true, Father can continue working on his irrigation system! And we can also sell the salt left over!"

"Well, if the prophecy doesn't come about for another few years, this irrigation system could make things a lot easier," Philo said.

"I hope it has the opportunity to do some good," Nicky sighed.

The Inner Laws

Fidus was once again walking down the dungeon stairs. Only this time he was carrying not only an orb of light, but also a plate of food. If it could be called that. The bread was stale and had been moldy a few minutes ago, but all of the mold had been cut off. There were two whole sardines, eyeballs and everything, and a small slab of tuna. The cup of water looked alright, but had a slight odor to it. Fidus had been told that the food was for the prisoner, but Fidus would be surprised if the Kale ate any of it. He told the guard by the door his business and who had sent him. He then made his way through the tunnel and to Norvus' cell.

"Hello again," Norvus greeted Fidus.

Fidus nodded in return, sliding the plate of food between two bars of the cell. The Kale took the food, sniffed it, and ate hungrily.

Fidus stared at him. "You're actually eating that?" he asked astonished.

The Kale looked up just as he swallowed the tuna. "It's all I have. This is my first meal since yesterday, after you left."

Fidus was once against bewildered. "But it's nearly mid-meal now. I left here almost twenty-four hours ago! Why haven't you been given any food?"

The Kale stared at him thoughtfully and asked, "Does that bother you?"

"Yes! I don't see why you should be treated this way. You have no way to do anything about it."

Norvus sat there, slowly swirling the water in the cup. "Are you treated like this?" he asked as he locked eyes with Fidus.

"No, of course not. I mean, I'm King Bacillus' apprentice so I'm given richer food than most apprentices. But even the weakest, most inexperienced is given better food than this." He motioned to the food with his hand and began pacing.

The Kale stared off into space. "Bacillus..." he muttered to himself. "I know that name... You know, you never told me your name. I did ask yesterday but you didn't answer me. Would you mind answering me now?"

"My name's Fidus."

"Tell me Fidus, do you know the Inner Laws?"

"Yes, of course, everyone knows them."

Norvus looked somewhat surprised. "Really? Even Bacillus?"

"We have to. King Bacillus even enforces such laws."

"Okay, what are they?"

Fidus began without hesitation. "We shall be loyal to no other king; do not use the kings name for evil, do not lie, do not steal--"

"Alright, you've proved you know the Inner Laws the way they've been taught to you. Here's the one thing I've noticed though. Bacillus has changed the word 'Creator' to 'king'."

"What's the difference? King Bacillus is both the creator of the Equalizers and our king."

"No, see, that's where you're confused. The word 'Creator' in the Inner Laws is referring to the Creator of all things, not just a particular city. Have you been taught the law 'you must not worship anyone but me'? The Creator wrote that, not Bacillus. By making the Inner Laws about himself, Bacillus has successfully made himself an idol."

"He has not!" Fidus stated, "He is here to lead us, not be worshiped by us!"

"Yes, but where is he leading you to?"

Fidus began speaking but stopped. He knew the answer, but had never vocalized it before. Finally deciding on how to word his answer, he said, "He's teaching us how to take Atlantis from the current king so he can rule it fairly. No one there is equal, and he wants to change that."

"That's not leading, that's using," the Kale stated flatly. 'That sentence just shows me Bacillus is in this for himself, not for any of his followers."

"That's a lie!" Fidus shouted. But even as his voice echoed through the room, he wondered if it was.

There was silence for a while, during which the Kale tried to chew the chunk of bread he had been given.

"Hmm," the Kale said thoughtfully as he continued to tear at the bread. "Another interpretation of a few of the Inner Laws is, treat others the same as you treat yourself."

"Yes, that's where King Bacillus thought of the name the Equalizers. Everyone here is to be treated equally."

Norvus put down the bread. "Then what about me?"

The question caught Fidus off guard. "What do you mean?"

"Why am I not treated equally?" Norvus clarified.

"Well, you're..." Fidus said, floundering for the right words, "not, one of us. You're not an Equalizer."

"Why should that matter? The Inner Law says 'treat others' not 'treat your friends,' or 'treat those like you.' Shouldn't I be treated the same?"

Fidus scowled, but did not reply. He could not find a good answer. The Kale, however, took his silence as an opening.

"Am I worthless simply because I live in a different place or have a different set of abilities?"

Fidus threw his hands in the air. "Stop it! Stop talking!" he shouted, "I'm sick of hearing your questions."

Norvus quieted down, but still looked as if he had something to say, which Fidus figured he probably did.

"Fine, we'll talk about something else," he said. "You guarding me must take time away from your studies, does it not?"

"Is it too much to ask for a little bit of silence?" Fidus snapped, still irritated with Norvus.

The Kale shrugged but continued to stare innocently at Fidus, obviously still waiting for an answer.

"Not really," Fidus said, finally giving in, "I study magic a little differently than most apprentices, since my master is the king. Once a week I go to him and he tells me what to do. My job is to figure out how and, if I can, practice that until the training session is over."

Shock was evident on the Kale's face.

"Are you serious?" he exclaimed.

"About what?"

"You're saying that Bacillus, your *master*, only *tells* you what spell to do but doesn't *show* you?"

Fidus laughed. "That's only if I'm lucky. He usually just tells me what he wants the result to look like. I have to figure out what spell and how to use it."

The Kale looked close to fainting.

"What's the problem?" Fidus asked.

"Do you have any idea how dangerous that is?" the Kale shouted, looking genially concerned, "There are so many ways a spell could go wrong! Every little thing has to be executed properly, the hand and staff position, the word choice, the amount of power used, even your thought process. Especially your thought process. Does he *want* you killed?"

A sick feeling suddenly settled in Fidus' stomach. "What do you mean killed? Can things go that wrong?"

"Yes, all kinds of things can happen! Things like fires being started on the apprentice's clothes, earthquakes at their feet, uncontrollable blinding lights, or the air in the room getting more difficult to breath. One apprentice somehow blinded himself, another one caused an explosion of lightning he couldn't control that nearly killed everyone in the room, and another created an illness that no one has found a cure for. When it comes to magic, you should never take a wild stab in the dark."

Fidus let out a shaky breath. No one had ever told him how dangerous magic could be. Not Bacillus, not other masters, no one. He knew of a few apprentices, and sometimes masters, who had suddenly disappeared, very few of which returned. He had been told they had been sent on missions. Had they actually been experimenting and have it go wrong?

"I remember my cousin trained as a sorcerer in the Palace when he was really young," Fidus said quietly, "When he was about ten he had an accident and scarred his hand badly. He was somehow able to sense danger because of it, but he was so frightened that he stopped practicing magic. I don't think he's stepped foot in a training room since."

Norvus closed his eyes, recalling an old memory. "I remember that. The sorcerers were afraid to try healing it, in fear of making it worse. No one knew what spells he had used and he hadn't known what he was doing. I didn't realize that was your cousin. Magic must run strong through your family."

"It does, through my mom's side. She used to tell me my ancestors were all powerful sorcerers. I guess my cousin got more magic since he was accepted to apprentice in the Palace and I never was." He spat out his last sentence with bitterness.

"Not necessarily," Norvus said gently. "The sorcerers might have all had apprentices when you were young enough. By the time your cousin was accepted you might have been considered too old."

"Why is being too old even an issue? If anything apprentices are accepted too young at the Palace. If they were older those types of accidents might not happen!"

"You would think that," Norvus sighed, "but the older the child, the more apt to experimenting they are. If we teach young children what to do and not to do, we can prevent most accidents from happening. It's not a perfect system, I'll give you that. But it's all we have right now."

Fidus decided to change the subject. "What about apprentices in Atlantis?" he asked, "What is their training session like?"

"The masters show their apprentices exactly how and when to do a spell. When they graduate from apprentice to sorcerer, they earn their staff. They are then walked through every spell they know with their new staff."

"Wait," Fidus held up his hand, "your apprentices don't get their staffs right away? We are given a staff the day we start training."

"I can't believe this," Norvus whispered to himself, "the crystal in the staff amplifies the user's power, as I'm sure you know. Our apprentices need to earn their staffs by proving they can handle their own power. Otherwise accidents would be far more common."

Fidus vaguely remembered being taught to work for things, but the concept was not practiced in the Underground Kingdom. If one person had something, everyone had it. It was another way to ensure fairness. As he thought about it though, it made more sense. If apprentices did not have a large amount of power, they could only do a small amount of damage. He decided to bring this to Bacillus' attention the next time they trained.

"So, how long are your training sessions Fidus?"

"Usually about fifteen minutes each," he replied, "Sometimes shorter if something comes up or I'm too weak to continue."

Fidus was getting used to the Kale's dumbfounded stares, so he was hardly surprised when it happened.

"But yesterday you told me you weren't allowed to practice magic outside of your training room," Norvus said unbelievingly.

"Yes..." Fidus confirmed slowly. He didn't have to wait long for Norvus to continue.

"Fifteen minutes a week? That's it? How can you be expected to remember anything? I can't believe this."

"What, Atlantis apprentices get more time than that?"

"Yes!" Norvus cried, "Three hours a day. Every day! That's just practicing spells!"

Fidus' head reeled. "Three hours a day? How do you have that kind of time?"

"What do you mean? What do you do all day that you don't have time for practice?"

"Well, every master is a little different, but usually the apprentices do different exercises in the health room until their master comes to take them for training. They train for however long the master says, then they go to the law room and memorize Bacillus' laws. Some of those are the Inner Laws."

"And what about you?"

"I'm in charge of the heath room. I make sure no apprentices come or go without permission. I also get them back on track if they get distracted, which doesn't happen often under my watch."

The Kale took a deep breath, trying to calm himself down. "What spells do you know?" His voice was a lot calmer now.

"I've mastered both the basics in combat magic and the element of light. I'm currently trying to master water."

"I can't believe you have mastered light with only fifteen minutes of practice a week," the Kale mumbled to himself.

"Are we still on that?" Fidus asked incredulous.

"Yes we are still on this! I can't believe the way you've been taught!"

"Don't insult what I'm being taught just because you have been taught something different!" Fidus yelled back, his anger instantly flooding back.

"Look at yourself Fidus!" Noruvs' pleading eyes focused on Fidus' flaming ones. "Look at the instructions you've been given! They are reckless and selfish and harmful. You have been living a lie, and just by listening to you I know you're smart enough to figure it out. Last night you didn't know how much your life is in danger on a day to day basis. Now you do. Look at your life Fidus, and tell me you can't make it better."

Fidus felt like he had been slapped in the face. No one had ever yelled at him and then told him that *he* could make his life better. He had never even been taught to think that. His face flushed with white hot anger. Before he knew what had happened, his hands were clenched in the air in front of the Kale. Water rushed into the cell. Rapids formed around the Kale. He was thrown to the floor, water flooding over him. Norvus began flailing his arms, trying to swim, but to no avail. It gathered around him until it formed a sphere, with him in the middle. The orb of water lifted off the ground and developed a current, spinning the Kale like a cyclone. Lights exploded in front of his eyes. He covered his face, trying to keep the water out of his mouth and nose. His breath was running out. His eyes squeezed shut.

Fidus suddenly realized what he was doing.

He rapidly stepped back, releasing his hold on the spell. The sphere dropped and exploded in a wave, the Kale sprawled out on the floor. When he had stopped the water spell, Fidus had also extinguished the lights. He quickly summoned enough light into a small orb and left it suspended in the air outside the cell. As the Kale spluttered and coughed, Fidus turned around and nearly ran to the stairs. Just before he reached them, he slowed his pace and slumped against the cold stone bars of the closest cell. He had never before been so angry that he lost control. He pressed his face against one of the bars, letting it pull the heat away from his cheek. His breathing slowed, and he slid to the floor, the Kale's cell to his left. What had just happened? He tried to remember. He had summoned enough water to completely cover the Kale, from where he was not sure, and had created a current. A pretty fast one too, judging by how fast Norvus was spinning. Fidus had then held at least five pulsating spheres of light by the Kale's eyes. Fidus glanced over at the Kale. He was still sprawled on the ground and was still coughing, but not as much. The man gingerly tried to push himself into a sitting position, but after a particularly harsh cough, ended up on his side. Fidus slowly stood and walked back to the flooded cell. When he got there, he knelt down by Norvus. Reaching through the bars, he helped him lean against them. Norvus pushed himself to the wall for a more comfortable position. He was about to say something when he curled up and began coughing again. Fidus closed his eyes and pictured the water in the Kale's lungs. He pulled the water together and out of the Kale's mouth. The coughing instantly stopped. Fidus opened his eyes and let the water fall to the floor.

Norvus was breathing heavily. "Why would you do that?" he asked finally. His voice was not harsh or accusing, but curious with just a hint of amazement.

"Do what?"

"Pull the water from my lungs."

Fidus turned his gaze away. "If I didn't you could have drowned. That's one of the Inner Laws, don't kill anyone." He sighed, "I've never lost control like that before."

"Of your anger, definitely, but you certainly didn't lose control of those spells."

Fidus was confused. "What do you mean? I completely lost control."

"No, losing control of a spell means it no longer does what you want. Those spells you cast did exactly what you wanted them to do, even if you didn't realize you wanted that."

Fidus realized Norvus was right. Even though it scared him to think that he had almost killed someone, he had been in control the whole time.

"Fidus," Norvus asked, the strength returning to his voice, "Have you ever done anything like that before?"

He stared at the floor as he shook his head. He felt too ashamed to even look the Kale in the eyes.

"So, Bacillus doesn't know your true power," Norvus replied, "Does he?"

Fidus sighed. "Until now even I didn't know." He looked at the Kale. "I've done a spell half as powerful as that before. After I had finished, Bacillus sent me away saying I was too weak to continue."

Norvus studied him. "Did you *feel* weak?" he asked.

"Well, not really. But King Bacillus summoned a mirror for me and when I saw myself I was paler than a pearl."

Norvus continued to study him. "You're not pale now," he stated simply. When a surprised look passed over Fidus' face Norvus said, "Do you *feel* weak now?"

"A little, I must be pale though."

"You're not. You said Bacillus summoned the mirror right?"

"Yes."

"Hmm…"

"What?"

"When I knew Bacillus as an apprentice he hated anyone with more power than himself. He always strived to be the best, and when that didn't make him more powerful, he made the other look weaker."

Fidus sighed. "You think he's making me appear weak?"

Norvus shrugged, but it was clear he thought it was definitely a possibility.

Fidus changed the subject. "You said you knew the King?"

Norvus nodded. "Tell me Fidus, do you know any of Bacillus' background?"

"Of course I do," Fidus replied, "He tells his story to everyone at least once a month to keep us inspired. His past is the reason we fight."

Norvus motioned for Fidus to continue.

"Well," Fidus began, "when King Bacillus was younger, he apprenticed in the Atlantis Palace as a sorcerer. As he grew, however, he became the most powerful sorcerer ever to live. His master knew this and was terrified of him. So he and all the other sorcerers threw him out of their counsel. It was then that King Bacillus realized that they were all greedy, self-centered power seekers. And people like that, who condemn those with more power should never be in charge. That's why he formed the Equalizers, to ensure equality throughout the Kingdom." Fidus sighed. *I don't tell it nearly as well has he does.*

"Wait, wait," the Kale said, waving his hands in the air. "That logic doesn't make any sense."

"What do you mean? It's perfectly logical!" Fidus argued. "He saw an injustice and set out to make it right."

"No, that's not what I meant," Norvus clarified, "The *story* is perfectly logical, not entirely true, but logical. And you should admire those who use their abilities and power to right a wrong. What confuses me is that, he says those who condemn people with greater abilities should never be a king. So, why is he condemning you?"

A small smile crept onto Fidus' face. Fidus had just saved the Kale in a way few could, and Norvus had just said people like that should be admired. He returned to the question on hand.

"He is far more powerful than I am. He condemning me is not the same thing as, say, me condemning him."

"When I knew Bacillus, he couldn't perform multiple spells that powerful at once, no matter what they were."

"Yes. He apprenticed as a King's sorcerer. He was chosen to apprentice because he was one of the most powerful for his age, not *the most powerful ever to live*, but powerful none the less. He was almost a graduated sorcerer, but something happened. As most people know, anyone serving in the Palace, the sorcerers, the scribes and even the royal family, have to follow the Inner and Requirement Laws. Well, Bacillus stopped following a few of them. We brought it to his attention, but he ignored us. He believed that he was better than the others."

"He is," Fidus interrupted.

The Kale began to speak, then stopped. He pressed his hands together, contemplated something, and tried again. "Let me rephrase that. Bacillus thought he was *worth* more than the others. He was definitely better *at* some things than some people, but he was not better *than* anyone else. Do you understand?"

"But, those are the same thing," Fidus answered.

"No they're not. You see, if abilities made someone better or worse than someone, which ability do you chose? You can't! There is no way! Everyone is different and unique and has hundreds of abilities. No two people are exactly the same, in either look or mind. Worth is not determined by ability or power. It is determined by being human, made by The Creator."

Fidus was not convinced. "Continue with your version of why my master is no longer a sorcerer in the Palace, if you please."

Norvus sighed, but continued the story. "As I was saying, he thought himself better than others. He even convinced other apprentices that one sorcerer was better than the other, when in reality we are all by the Requirement Laws equals. If one was superior to another, it would start fights for power. But he decided that he would rule Atlantis by collecting followers and overthrowing the King and anyone else who stood in his way. Of course we couldn't let this happen. We warned him three times to change. He refused each time, so we had no choice but to relieve him of apprenticeship."

"Well, if you tried to discourage him, it didn't work," Fidus bragged. "He still plans to overthrow Atlantis."

"With you by his side?" Something in his gaze made Fidus hesitate.

"Well, of course," Fidus replied uncertainly.

"How can you tell? By what you told me he only keeps you around to keep order in the health room. He knows how to train apprentices, he knows what works. He obviously isn't doing this for you. Has it ever occurred to you that he is simply keeping you close to watch you? Can't you see that he thinks you might be a threat?"

He had no idea how to answer the Kale. Fidus glanced at the water clock by the wall. He sighed with relief when he saw his time to guard the Kale was over.

"I have to go," he said simply. He stood and began walking away.

"Think about it," Norvus called after him.

Fidus looked over his shoulder, and extinguished the light.

That small seed of doubt had now blossomed.

Tarts and Sticky Feet

"So, is there anything I should expect when we meet your uncle?" Nicky asked Philo. After they left the Palace, they had headed to his uncle's house, located in the Rus' realm. And now they were almost there.

"He's not crazy, if that's what you mean," Philo reassured Nicky.

"No, I didn't mean it like that. It's just that, well, you said he never goes outside."

"And I also told you that the reason he stays in his house all the time is because he just doesn't like the way people look at him when he says he wrote farm labels for a living. I know, it's a bit extreme, but that's just the way he is."

"But he lives in the Rus' realm. The two farm realms are on either side. I mean, I would understand if he lived in the Sem's realm, which is all mountain terrain, but in the Rus' realm is writing labels for farmers really that strange? I would think lots of people write labels there."

"Oh they do," Philo explained, "but it's usually a person's first job or side job, not his life job. Like, when I come to age in four years, I might do that to gather some money until I figure out what trade I would like to pursue. But once I find out what gift of mine I want to follow, I would quit writing labels. Uncle Berum thinks it makes him look lazy or inadequate, like he never took the time to find a real trade to follow. My family's told him otherwise, but he refuses to listen."

Nicky sighed, reminiscing. When Philo said he was coming to age in four years, it reminded her how long she had really known him. She thought back to the day that she had first met him, when his oldest brother had graduated from apprentice to sorcerer. She had been five at the time, and he had been six. They had become really close friends when Philo and his friends had taught her how to play Quibthrow, four years later.

By now they had reached the house. It was similar to every other house in the village Philo lived in, with brown, clay walls and a similar roof. The only exception was that it was a good distance away from the nearby village, surrounded by a garden that contained plants of all sorts. There were tomatoes, grapes, mushrooms, pumpkins, watermelon, and enough other plant species to make Philo wonder if his uncle's house was considered its own farm. Another difference was the walkway of different colored bricks leading up to the front door, which was lined with strawberry, blueberry and raspberry bushes. He did not remember the berry bushes from the last time he had visited, but that had been in winter, when the berries were out of season. When Philo and Nicky stepped onto the bricks, he could tell that they were not painted. His feet stuck to some parts and, when he lifted his foot, it was the color he had just stepped on. "Careful," he warned Nicky, "these bricks are a little sticky." Another thing was the irregularity of the brick colors. Some bricks were dyed three different colors, while others were not dyed at all. Then, a split second before he did, Nicky understood and exclaimed with delight, "Look! They've been dyed by all the different berry bushes! See? Those blue bricks are by the blueberry bushes, those red ones are next to the strawberries, and the purple ones by the raspberries!"

A smile grew on Philo's face as he realized she was right. He always enjoyed Nicky's excitement when she figured something out.

Now that they knew that the dye was really berry juice, they were careful to step on clean bricks to keep their feet from getting sticky. While they were jumping from brick to brick, they would point out clear places for the other to step. About half way to the door, Philo had gotten ahead of Nicky and, in an attempt to catch up, she leaped forward so she was even with him, but lost her balance. She tottered, her feet rooted to the spot, hoping to keep her feet clean. She looked around wildly for another place to put her feet, but could not find one and began to fall, all the while flailing her arms around looking quite ridiculous. It was all Philo could do to keep from laughing as she fell towards him. In once swift movement he caught her and helped her regain her balance. Once she had regained her footing, she covered her face with her hands and turned away in exaggerated embarrassment.

"That could have been avoided," she said, her voice muffled from her hands.

Philo chucked and she peeked out at him from between her slender fingers.

"Well now you know not to race me," Philo stated in mock seriousness.

"Who said anything about racing?" Nicky asked innocently, a hint of a smile at the edges of her mouth.

"It's always a race."

"Oh really?" Nicky laughed. Even as she said this, she sprinted down the brick path, nimbly jumping from one plain brick to the next.

Philo grinned as he raced after her.

They reached the door nearly at the same time, slightly out of breath. After his heart had calmed down to its usual pace, at least as normal as it could be when he was around Nicky, he raised his hand and knocked on the door.

"Hello? Uncle Berum? It's Philo!"

He heard a rustling inside a few moments before the door swung open. He was just as Philo remembered. A short, thin man with a full head of grey hair. He wore a long, brown robe fastened with a green sash at his waist. His face broke into a smile, exposing his nearly perfect white teeth. His eyes looked over Philo before turning to Nicky.

"Good morning, Princess," he addressed her, bowing slightly as he inclined his head.

Nicky greeted him as well before he turned back to Philo.

"Good morning, Philo," he said to him, although not as formally. "How have you been?"

"I've been well, thank you."

"And what be the reason for you stopping by? If you were alone I would assume it would be just to say hello. But the princess being here tells me your visit is of more important matters. Am I right?"

Philo held up his hand, motioning for Nicky to speak. She had never said why she wanted to see his uncle, so she had to answer for herself.

Nicky glanced around and replied in a low voice, "It's about a prophecy I need help solving."

Philo spun his head around to stare at her. *A prophecy?* He thought, astonished. *Why would she need my uncle's help with a prophecy when she has so many other, more-qualified sorcerers to question.*

A hint of eagerness hit his uncle's eyes. "A prophecy? I wonder... Come in, come in. Let us discuss this in more detail." He ushered them in the house and shut the door. Once inside, he moved swiftly down the hall, calling over his shoulder that they could sit in a room off to the right. Philo and Nicky looked around. When they had entered the doorway they had stepped on a soft mat with small berry juice stains. Neither Philo nor Nicky knew where to go since they were reluctant to walk farther down the hall while they still had sticky feet, until

Berum announced they could remove the berry juice with the reed mat they stood on. The two friends wiped their feet and walked into the room Berum had pointed out previously.

The room had not changed since Philo had been there last, about a month before. In the center of the room stood a low table, surrounded by four wooden chairs with multi-colored pillows on the seats. There were two windows on one wall, and a doorway leading to the back of the house on another. Paintings of various sizes hung on every wall, most of which Philo knew his uncle had painted himself. A large, blue reed mat covered most of the floor and there was a water clock in the far right corner. Philo and Nicky each took a chair opposite of each other as they continued to look around. They did not need to wait long for Berum to return. He entered the room carrying a plate of fruit pastries and cups of water. He set them on the table and sat down in one of the remaining chairs. He motioned the young adults to help themselves to the treats, taking one himself. Philo bit into a delicious flakey sphere filled with raspberry. Berum allowed them a few bites before asking, "So, tell me more of this prophecy and why you're coming to me, not a Palace Scribe?"

Nicky swallowed a bite from her strawberry pastry and spread out the scroll she had tucked into the sash around her waist and handed it to Berum.

"This is a prophecy that I need help unraveling. The King's Sorcerers believe it predicts the end of Atlantis, but don't know what the rest means. I need help figuring out *how* exactly Atlantis will fall, if that is truly what the prophecy is about. That is why I came to you. I've already discussed this prophecy with my father's best sorcerers and scribes, but they're all as confused as I am. I was hoping that you would know someone who can help me, if you can't yourself."

"How did you think to come to me?" the man asked.

"Philo mentioned that you were a scribe and I thought you might be able to help."

"I see. Well, why didn't you ask one of the Palace Scribes for help?"

Nicky glanced down at her hands which rested on her lap. "By the time I thought of asking one of them, the Palace Scribes were already really annoyed with me."

Berum raised an eyebrow. "Why is that?"

"I'd rather not go into detail."

The man shrugged and looked down at the scroll, which he then began to read.

Philo had been watching the conversation with confusion and disbelief. He did not know how to react to Nicky keeping the possible downfall of Atlantis a secret from him. There had been a time when they had told each other everything, from a strange number of petals on a flower they found, to a new secret they discovered, to the story they had just made up. If it was important to one, it was important to the other. Nicky glanced up at him and noticed the questioning look on his face. "I waited until now so I only had to reveal the prophecy once," she explained, "If I had to repeat it, the chances of someone overhearing me would have gone up. It's safer this way."

Now Philo understood. He felt bad for doubting Nicky. She smiled at him and he knew he was forgiven.

"I remember this," Berum sighed, placing the unrolled scroll on the table. Philo arched his neck to get a better look at the writing.

"What do you mean 'you remember'?" Nicky asked suspiciously. "You've read this before?"

Philo finished reading and glanced up at his uncle.

The man sighed again as he leaned forward, resting his head on his chest. To Philo, it looked as if his uncle was deciding upon the best course of action. Finally, after both Philo and Nicky were barely able to keep themselves from wriggling impatiently in their chairs, Berum spoke.

"Yes, I have read this before."

"Before you retired?"

"Yes."

Nicky looked as if something had just occurred to her. "How long ago was this prophesy written?" She exclaimed.

Berum tilted back his head as he tried to remember. "About five, six years ago? Yes, around that time."

Nicky gawked. How had the sorcerers kept the prophesy hidden for that long?

"Princess, what trade did my nephew say I practiced?"

"Scribing. You wrote labels for various farms," she replied, "Is that not true?"

"No, it is true," he answered, "At least, for some of my life. Do you know what else I did?" This time he was asking both Nicky and Philo. When they both shook their heads, Berum leaned forward. The young adults also drew closer, almost without meaning to.

In a low voice, as if he was afraid of eavesdroppers, said, "I was a scribe for the Oracle herself." He let the words hang in the air as he once again sat back in his chair. Philo and Nicky, however, remained in the same position, leaning forward with their arms on their knees. They both turned to look at each other, disbelieving. Oracle Scribes were by law required to remain undiscovered, for they were the only ones, besides the King and Queen, who knew the exact location of the Oracle. If an Oracle Scribe reviled who he was, someone opposing the King could force the Oracle's location from the scribe and use it to his own advantage, which was very dangerous. The Oracle's prophesies were only revealed to the people they concerned and never to the public. The reason for this was people would interpret the prophesy their own way, and then act accordingly. The correct interpretation was rarely the same, and there had almost always been disastrous results.

Philo sat back in his chair. He viewed his uncle in an entirely different way now. Instead of paranoid, self-conscience, and practically a hermit, he saw him as a sort of spy. A man who was secretive by law, and doing everything he could to keep his identity from being compromised.

"An Oracle's Scribe..." Nicky repeated, almost to herself. "Huh! What luck that you end up being an Oracle's Scribe!"

"I don't believe in luck," Berum stated, "I believe in blessings."

Nicky shrugged, but continued. "You're an Oracle's Scribe who's said that he's read the prophesy in question before. Did you by any chance copy it yourself?"

"What do you mean by copy it?" Philo asked. Being from the village, he knew very little about the Oracle. He was still under the impression that she was a pale old witch.

Berum quickly explained how the prophesies were recorded.

"No, I didn't write this particular one down. I did, however, take the place of the one who did."

"Take the place?"

The man lowered his eyes and replied with a sad tone, "Yes. There is an unfortunate side effect of hearing a prophesy as it's being spoken. Anyone who hears a prophesy as the Oracle speaks it is affected in ways no one understands. Some lose their hearing, others fall into a deep sleep and don't awaken for a long time. But something happens to almost every one that makes them feel like they *must* find the answer to the prophesy, figure out what every riddle means. This, of course is nearly impossible until the event has passed. They devote all their time and energy to the task and, eventually, they go insane. This is the case of Teneo, the man who heard this particular prophesy."

Nicky also cast down her gaze. Philo's blueberry tart seemed to have lost all flavor.

"And nothing can be done to help these people?" Nicky asked.

"Not that we know of," Philo's uncle replied. "Thankfully, it has only happened five times in our history, and there have been dozens of prophesies in that time."

Philo spoke up. "Well, that's good."

"So, that answers a question you asked me a few minutes after we had met. He's the best person I know that can help you."

"Where can we find him?"

"At the border of the Cor and Rus realms, about a half hour walk from here. He lives in a house with two floors with a flower garden wrapped around the entire building, mostly anemones."

"Do you know if he'll be there?" Philo asked.

"Yes, he'll be there. He doesn't leave his room. You'll be greeted by his guard."

The word guard gave Nicky a feeling of uneasiness, but she pushed it aside for now.

"Thank you," Nicky said instead, "You've been a great help. But you're still an Oracle's Scribe. Do you at least have an opinion on what this prophecy means?"

"I'm afraid not. That's something I try to avoid actually. I prefer not to dwell on something that I have no way of altering. "

"You mean you don't have *any* thoughts on the subject?"

Berum shook his head.

"Well, thank you again for your help. You said he lives at the border of the Cor and Rus realms?"

"Yes. Do you need me to show you the way?"

"No, I think we can manage. Thank you for the offer though."

Philo grabbed a blackberry tart and said good bye to his uncle, promising to visit him again soon. Berum showed them to the door and bade them farewell. Before they left he said, "Now remember, when you came here I was just a label scribe, nothing more. Keep my secret safe, alright?"

Philo and Nicky swore themselves to secrecy and started down the path. Berum bade them farewell and the two young adults waved over their shoulders until the wood door was shut behind them.

They had walked for a few minutes before Philo split the tart down the middle and offered a half to Nicky. She accepted and asked, "Are you ready for this?" She did not ask if Philo would be joining her; she knew by the look on his face that he was.

"I hope so," he replied. He had read the prophesy and was a little worried what they would find out. But something told him that he had to be there. Besides, he had never seen a truly insane person before and was a bit curious.

"I sure hope so," he repeated under his breath, taking a bite out of the tart.

Possibilities

"So, what do you think we should expect?" Nicky did not want to admit it, but she was nervous about meeting Teneo, the one who had heard the prophecy as it was spoken.

"Sorry Nicky, I don't have a clue. I've never really encountered anyone who was actually insane. I mean, I've met people who did not exactly have a full grasp on reality, as I think everybody has, but not someone who had to be locked up because of it."

"Hmm…" His answer did not exactly reassure her, but she continued walking. The long grass had completely taken the sticky feeling away from their feet, and for that Nicky was grateful. She had been worried someone might have seen their feet sticking to the cobblestone roads and wondered what they had stepped in. Not Philo though. He never worried about what others thought of him or wondered how they were judging him. He went through life, both the ups and downs, with confidence. It did not matter if he fell in a stream or someone dropped a bucket of paint on his head. If it was an accident, he would laugh it off and walk on. *How does he do it?* Nicky wondered. She could never trip or fall without fearing who saw it. Then again, she was the Princess. What she did was what people talked about. If she helped build something important, or knocked over a plate of eggs, people would remember. But she still wished she could have Philo's attitude towards things like that. She sighed. *Just one more thing to admire him for.*

"Hey Nicky, could you hand me the scroll?" Philo asked.

She complied and he began to read.

"What do you think '*Although life will seem to disappear, Atlantis subjects will still be here*' means?" he said after a while.

"I don't know," she replied. After thinking about it though, she said, "Maybe the sorcerers will put a spell over the island that makes it invisible to people on the other side."

Philo nodded. "That could happen. Maybe the reason for the spell is to protect us against the '*enemy that had once been friend*'."

"Maybe..." Nicky suddenly turned to Philo. "I just realized something! If Teneo has been trying to figure out what the prophecy means since it was spoken, that means he's been obsessing over it for six years!"

Philo whistled. "No wonder he's crazy. I would be too if I couldn't find the answer to a puzzle for that long."

"Can you imagine?" Nicky asked almost in a whisper, "thinking about nothing else for six years? Never even leaving your room?"

"My uncle says he doesn't leave his room and that he also has a guard. Do you think he's..."

"Been locked up?" Nicky finished in horror. "For something he couldn't help? No! He couldn't be locked away! He would be there on his own free will. Unless he's dangerous... You don't think he's dangerous do you?"

"I guess we'll find out," Philo stated.

It was probably not the best path they could have chosen, walking in to visit Teneo with next to no information. They knew he never left his room, he had a guard, and was insane. And although she did not act like it, Nicky was losing confidence that this was a wise plan, not that she did the wisest thing very often. Philo figured he should get her mind off of the potentially dangerous meeting.

"Hey Nicky, come look over here!" He pointed over to a field a few paces to their left where various crops were growing. He walked over to a row of cotton saplings. A thin copper pipe on a shallow angle was propped above the plants, which he began to follow up its incline. He turned and saw Nicky following him, keeping her steady gaze on the pipe. As they continued to walk, the pipe grew in height. When they had started following it the pipe had been touching the ground, since they had begun their trip at the edge of the field. The pipe had just passed eye level when Nicky mentioned, "there are no seams on the pipe. Whoever made this pipe used magic."

"You're right. Do you think the maker of this pipe summoned the copper to form it or just fused together pipes that were already made?" He reached out and loosely grasped the smooth metal, letting his hand run over the smooth metal. It suddenly began vibrating, if only ever so slightly. A vague chill ran from Philo's hand up to his shoulder. He pulled back his arm, and a moment later water streamed out of tiny holes punched into the pipe's underside. Nicky let out a laugh of recognition.

"Aha! It *is* my father's irrigation system! And it works just the way he said it would!" She took off down the rows of crops towards the beginning of the pipe. Philo quickly caught up to her as she neared her destination. There, a few feet above their heads, was the beginning of the pipe with a funnel attached to it. Philo watched as a man who was standing on a ladder poured water down the funnel.

"See? The water flows down the pipe and through the holes! But the holes are too small to take all the water at once, so it goes down the pipe and waters the rest of the plants! And Father even got a funnel made! Isn't it amazing?"

"It is." Philo's plan to get Nicky's mind on a different track, even if briefly, had worked.

They found their way back to the path and shortly came to a house surrounded with anemone flowers. There was something about them that Nicky instantly liked. The soft, delicate flowers painted with blues and violets gave her a sense of calmness. As they walked up the path Nicky bent down to rub the petals between her fingers.

"Can I help you?"

Nicky quickly stood, smoothing her dress. The soft voice had come from the woman who now stood in the doorway. She wore a simple white dress that came down to her ankles, and her long hair tied back. Even though she appeared to be in her late thirties, her hair was completely grey.

"Yes," Nicky replied as the nervous feeling began to return. "We're looking for a man named Teneo. We were told he lives here."

"And why do you wish to see him, Princess?"

"We need to talk to him about the… uh, the prophecy." Nicky was painfully aware that bringing up the prophecy might not be something she should do. But if she had brought up a dangerous subject, the woman did not show it.

"I see. My name is Rachel. Please, come in." She backed into the house to make room for Nicky and Philo to enter. The room was simply furnished with a few large pillows positioned around a low table and a window on the far wall. Rachel led them through a doorway to their right and up a flight of stairs. When they reached the top, they faced a closed wooden door.

"When you enter this room, be very careful not to ruin anything he has written. Watch where you step, sit, or what you lean up against." With that, Rachel knocked surprisingly loudly on the door, waited a few seconds, and pushed it open. Nicky and Philo were ushered inside and the door shut behind them. Nicky stared at what was inside. The entire room was covered with writing. The walls, floor, and even the ceiling had been drawn on. Piles of parchment were stacked in a corner, each one black from the amount of charcoal that had been rubbed on them. Then they saw him. He sat on the floor in a far corner with his head in his hands. Like Philo, he wore a long shirt that was halfway to his knees with a belt around his waist and loose pants. The two friends carefully approached him. As they got closer they heard him murmuring under his breath.

Nicky could just barely hear him repeating a line from the prophecy when he looked up and ran his charcoal coated fingers through his hair, leaving long black streaks.

"Why are you here?"

He did not sound the way Nicky had imagined. His kind voice was soft and level, nothing wild about it.

"We came to see if you could help us with the prophecy," Nicky replied.

"Or if we could help you," Philo added.

A look of recognition crossed Teneo's face. "The prophecy..." He stood and walked across the room, automatically avoiding stepping on tiles that had been drawn on. He walked to a bookshelf, the open door had obstructed it from Nicky's view, and took a book that he began flipping through franticly.

Philo and Nicky followed him slowly as they tried to find the exact path Teneo had taken so as to not smudge the charcoal. When they had gotten closer they could hear him murmuring, "They ask about the prophecy... They ask about the prophecy..." over and over, rapidly turning pages.

When he had flipped through about half the book he suddenly slammed it shut and exclaimed "The prophecy! *Conquered by enemy that had once been friend, the king's reign will come to an end. His family will meet, all but one, for she will see a quivering sun. Much will crash without sound, and some will fall yet hit no ground. From this disaster will come a tale, one handed down without a fail. Although life will seem to disappear, Atlantis subjects will still be here. The city will crumble yet not decay, if the sorcerers can find a way. All will lie on them to mend, assisted by enemy that is now friend."*

"Yes, that's the one I'm talking about," Nicky replied, a bit taken aback by his behavior. Then again, what did she expect?

"What do you wish to learn?"

"Anything you know."

"I know nothing," he replied, setting the book back on the shelf, all the while keeping his eyes on Nicky. "I only guess. What part of the prophecy do you wish to discuss?"

"How about we start at the beginning?" Philo spoke up. He asked Nicky for the scroll and began to read. *"Conquered by enemy that had once been friend, the king's reign will come to an end.'* So, a previously friendly nation attacks us and takes over?"

"Maybe. Maybe not," Teneo replied, his wide eyes now fastened on Philo, "The enemy that had once been friend might refer to a nation that is ruled by the king's family. The enemy could also be a friend of the king personally who takes over. Another interpretation might be the heir to the throne might kill the king as to take over."

Nicky gasped. She was the only one considered an heir to the throne. "I wouldn't harm my own father!" She nearly yelled with shock. "Besides, if someone even tried to kill him they wouldn't measure up to the code! That whole 'you must never kill anyone' part, that's what has kept our rulers safe through the years!"

"You can't really believe that Nicky would do that," Philo exclaimed.

"I don't," Teneo replied, "but it is nevertheless a possibility. Remember, this prophecy was spoken six years ago and may not come to pass for another ten. This prophecy might not be about you." He turned back to Philo. "The enemy that had once been friend might be symbolic. The enemy might not be a nation, a single person, or even human." He crossed the room and pointed at something written on a wall. "The enemy might be something like horses. We use them to ride across the island to deliver news faster, to pull wagons, for farm work. They are our friends in that sense. Someone might make one angry and cause a stampede, destroying plants, small animals, and slow people. That would be one explanation of line five, *'Although life will seem to disappear, Atlantis subjects will still be here.'*"

Nicky and Philo glanced at each other. There were more possible outcomes in a single line then they had thought for the whole prophecy.

Philo walked over to Teneo and studied the writing he was pointing at. It was a list of things like cattle, sorcerers, nations that traded goods, the subjects themselves, anything that could be considered a friend.

"Earth is listed here," Philo mentioned. "How could the earth turn against us?"

"An earthquake," Teneo answered softly. "We farm for food and mine for precious metals. An earthquake could destroy farmland, causing the nation to starve, or the mines, which could cause a financial collapse. Both are ways line six could come about."

"The city will crumble yet not decay, if the sorcerers can find a way," Philo read from the scroll.

Nicky, who still uneasy at the thought of her killing her own father even being discussed, wanted desperately to change the subject. "So you're saying," she began, addressing Teneo, "that nothing in the prophecy should be taken literally?"

"Some things should," Teneo corrected, "but some things should not."

"How about the next line?" Philo asked, *"His family will meet, all but one, for she will see a quivering sun?"*

Teneo walked briskly over to another part of the room and stared at a floor tile in the corner of the room near Nicky. "The girl in the prophecy could be under water when she looks at the sun. Another possibility is the family in the prophecy might come here on a ship with a large sail which, if the sun was seen through it, would give it a quivering effect."

"That must mean the prophecy will start late in the day," Philo said, thinking aloud.

Nicky looked at him quizzically, "What do you mean? How can you possibly know what time?"

"Well, the ships the royal family travel on are very large," he began. "The large ships dock on the west side of the island, and if the girl looks through the sail to see the sun, the sun must be low in the sky. A sun low in the sky to the west means late in the day."

"Maybe not," Teneo spoke up. "The girl might be closer to the ship than what you're thinking, therefore the sun might be higher in the sky. Or the girl might not even be on the island, she could be on the ship itself. If that is true there is really no way to tell the time."

Philo agreed, but looked disappointed that his theory could be proven unstable so quickly.

"But a very interesting idea," Teneo continued. He pulled a stick of charcoal out from a fold in his belt, kneeled to the floor, and began writing down what Philo had said. When Nicky glanced back at Philo he looked happier. She smiled, happy to see him happy, and turned back to Teneo. His hair had fallen into his face and he had brushed it aside, leaving streaks of charcoal in his hair. There on the wall near his head was a picture he had drawn. Nicky bent down to get a better look.

The drawing was of a kingdom, the Palace in the background at the very center. At the right of the Palace was a volcano and a forest, and to the left were villages. Smaller buildings had been drawn in front of the Palace with tiny marks that resembled people on the ground. Nicky was not sure, but it looked like they were all running towards the right of the kingdom. Up in the left corner was a disk with arcs following it, giving it the appearance it was falling. Above the whole thing was the number two.

"Teneo, what's this picture mean?"

He knelt down next to her and looked to where she was pointing.

"Another possibility for line two. This is Atlantis," he pointed to the kingdom, "and this is the sun," his finger moved to the falling disk. "When the family meets, the girl might look up and see the sun falling. If the sun falls from the sky, like the rock that became our island, our crops will wither, the ground will be burned and dented, and many people could die. The sun could be bent from its circular form and cease to give us light."

Nicky had never thought about the sun falling. She had always been told the small disk that gave them light was wedged in the sky too tight it could never fall. "How big of an impact do you think the sun would make if it did fall from the sky?" Nicky asked.

"Our island left a huge crater, which you can see from underwater. If the sun fell, it could make a dent in the earth as wide as the Palace, but it's doubtful it would cause a crater any larger since it's so small. But the sun gives us light and heat, so if the heat comes closer people might burn, and if the light goes out the crops will die."

"If the sun fell, life all over the world would be harmed. Everyone requires the sun! Is there any way we can prevent that from happening?" Philo asked desperately.

Nicky glanced at him then back at Teneo. Her father had said prophecies came true no matter what, but she did not know if you could prevent a particular possibility.

"Yes," Teneo replied, "but it can be very difficult and sometimes preventing one outcome results in something worse."

Nicky stared at the picture. "It seems someone should at least try to keep this one from happening. Seeing the sun through a ship's sail is a lot better than holding it in your hands."

"Someone did once," Teneo stated simply, "try to prevent the sun from falling."

"When?" Philo asked, followed immediately by Nicky asking, "How?"

"A year after the prophecy had been spoken," Teneo started, "Three sorcerers came to see me, asking about the prophecy. I told them about this outcome and they decided to prevent it. They went outside and one of them, the one who had mastered light, created a platform and flew into the sky. His plan was to see what held the sun in the sky and if it could be made stronger. He flew so high up that we lost sight of him. After a while, we saw something falling. It was him. He was about to crash into the ocean when the sorcerer who had mastered air summoned wind to ease his fall. He hit the water and broke his back. When they rescued him, his hands had frostbite, ice was on his clothes, and he was unconscious. After he awoke, he said the closer you got to the sun, the colder it got. Eventually it got so cold he couldn't breathe, and lost consciousness. No one ever attempted to reach the sun again. It was too dangerous."

They sat in silence, thinking about the story.

"Why would it get colder the closer you got to the sun?" Nicky asked, "That doesn't make any sense."

"Would that mean that, if the sun fell, the ground might freeze instead of burn?" Philo wondered.

Teneo simply shook his head and walked away.

Philo's eyes wandered around the room. "We're getting off track. What's this picture with the three by it mean?"

He pointed to a picture of a person, a sorcerer, with wavy lines coming from his open mouth.

"The number three means line three," Teneo stated as he made his way over to them.

Philo glanced at the scroll. *"Much will crash without sound, and some will fall yet hit no ground,"* he read.

"If we are attacked by sorcerers," Teneo explained, "one thing they might do is attack with a deafening noise, like a scream. Everyone might go momentarily deaf, and in that moment things might fall and appear to have no noise."

"What about the second part?" Nicky brought up, turning away from a list written on the wall. "The part where people will fall but not hit the ground."

"The sorcerers might cast a spell that keeps things suspended in the air, either to capture the kingdom more easily, or to save us from the impact of falling."

"So, if this list I'm looking at has a three next to it," Nicky said, turning back to the wall, "does that mean it's about line three also?"

"Yes," he pointed to a sentence. "Some other noise besides a scream might overpower the sound of things crashing, like a large windstorm or a huge wave. Or the prophecy might come to pass in the far future where only people who cannot hear remain. Or maybe the prophecy will happen at night when everyone is asleep, so they don't hear anything."

Nicky sat back on her heels. This was a lot more information than she had thought they would get.

Just then Rachel who had brought them to Teneo entered the room.

"Will you be staying for mid-meal?" she asked Philo and Nicky.

Nicky had glimpsed the kitchen on her way up the stairs. Small, with only a few cupboards. If Nicky and Philo stayed it would probably be a stretch for her.

"No, we're actually going to the marketplace for mid-meal," Nicky replied.

"We also need to buy some paper so we can take some notes with us," Philo put in.

Rachel's shoulders relaxed ever so slightly.

"Very well," she said, "Teneo, come down to the kitchen to eat please." He crossed the room and began walking down the stairs. She turned back to Nicky. "We will finish eating in twenty minutes, you may come back then."

"Thank you, is there anything we can get for you in the market?"

"No, I go to the marketplace tomorrow. You don't need to trouble yourself."

She lead the them down the stairs to the front door. They said goodbye and walked to the market.

The Question of Loyalty

Fidus had requested to be seen by Bacillus. He stood in a hallway arguing with an emergency messenger. Except for emergency situations, no one but Bacillus decided when people were admitted into his presence; everyone knew that. Only spies and Masters of Masters could request an audience with Bacillus at any time. But not a lowly apprentice. Fidus asking to be seen without being summoned was so unorthodox that the messenger who handled all of Bacillus' affairs was struck dumb.

"Uh, wh-- what exactly is the nature of this, er, request to be summoned?" the messenger asked, slowly regaining use of his voice.

"Tell my Master and King, Bacillus, that I wish to speak with him about our prisoner," Fidus stated.

The messenger still looked uncertain, but ran to deliver the message.

Fidus hoped Bacillus would accept.

After a half hour of waiting, Fidus grew bored. There was no telling when he would receive an answer, if Bacillus even decided it was worth his time to send one. He began looking around. Down the hall, the tunnel let out into the ocean, the water held out by a spell. Fidus loved these windows. He walked over to it and sat down, staring out into the ocean. Up at the surface he could just make out a fishing boat. A boat from Atlantis.

Fidus sighed. Most of what the Kale had said was so opposite from everything Fidus knew that he didn't know what to think. He hoped, nearly prayed, that Bacillus could help sort out what was to be believed and what was to be ignored. One thing that stuck out in his mind was Norvus saying that experimenting with spells was dangerous. Fidus could definitely see how it could be deadly. What if he had encased *himself* in a sphere of water instead of the Kale? But Fidus had experimented for nearly his entire apprenticeship, and he was still alive. He looked around again, no sign of the messenger, or anyone else for that matter. He looked back into the water. Taking a deep breath, he reached his hand in and pulled out an orb of water, the chill running down his arms. He slowly molded the water into different shapes. First a sphere, then a cylinder, then a square. He quickly studied his reflection in the wall of water. He looked completely normal, not the slightest bit pale. Beyond his reflection, he saw a school of fish swim by. He turned back to the water in his hands. With just a bit of excitement, he began to mold the water into the shape of a fish. He obtained the basic outline immediately, then began working on the details. He imagined scales, fins, and eyes. They all began to appear on the fish. He smiled as he held it up for inspection. Rotating the hand-sized fish in midair, he kept adding small details. He had never done anything so small and intricate before. He suddenly remembered, back when he was five, he had gotten a lump of clay for his birthday. He had molded and remolded that bit of clay for an entire year. Molding water was much more fun. A sudden inspiration hit him. He erased the fish and began sculpting a dolphin, taking more water from the ocean to make it larger. It quickly grew to the length of his forearm. When he had finished, its transparency and size were the only differences between it and a real dolphin. Fidus closed his eyes, concentrating on the way a dolphin swims. The dolphin left his hands and, when he opened his eyes, it was swimming around the hall. A triumphant smile lit up his face. He was not smiling because he had proved experimenting was not always dangerous, he was smiling because he had done something no one else had thought of, and he wasn't the slightest bit tired or pale. He looked back at his reflection just to be sure. A strong, healthy sorcerer stared back at him.

He let the dolphin swim around for a little while longer before drifting it back into the ocean. The moment it was in water the effort it took to keep its shape drastically increased. Fidus immediately pulled it back into the hallway, letting out a small gasp. The sudden demand of energy had caught Fidus off guard. *That must be what Norvus was talking about,* he thought to himself with a grim smile. Concentrating on keeping the water pulled together, Fidus slowly pushed it back into the ocean. Once again it immediately wanted to lose form, but Fidus was determined. Unfortunately, so was the ocean. It seemed bent on claiming the water-dolphin as its own once more. Fidus quickly pulled the dolphin back from the ocean. He stared out at the sea, then back to the dolphin, a course of action beginning to form in his mind. He knew he had to keep the ocean away from the dolphin... But how? Air was the only thing he could think of... create a bubble around the dolphin. He thought back to his one and only lesson in air manipulating. As he eased the dolphin back through the window, he pushed the water away from it in the form of a bubble. There was still the effort of containing the air, but not nearly as much as before. He let the dolphin swim around within its bubble for a while longer before releasing the air and letting his creation dissolve into the surrounding sea. Fidus glanced back at his reflection. He was flushed with excitement. For the five years of apprenticeship he had worked with magic, but had not been able to enjoy it. He leaned against the wall and closed his eyes, truly happy for the first time in a long time.

✳✳✳

Fidus was just growing bored again when the messenger he had sent to Bacillus arrived. Fidus stood as the messenger spoke.

"King Bacillus has granted your request to be summoned," the man said simply.

Sighing with relief, Fidus thanked the man and quickly walked down the tunnel towards his master's chambers.

He soon arrived, said the proper spell to open the hidden door, and walked inside.

"Hello, Apprentice," Bacillus greeted with a small note of irritation to his voice.

"Hello, Master," Fidus replied as he bowed at the waist.

Bacillus ignored him for a time, clearly stating that he could use Fidus' time in any way he pleased. Finally, without looking up from the paper he was writing, he told Fidus to explain why he had been so eager to come.

"It has to do with our prisoner the Kale," Fidus immediately dove into the story as he sat down on a wooden chair. "You see, he's been saying things that contradict everything I've been taught."

"Lies, all lies," Bacillus instantly stated without looking up.

"Well you see, Master, I'm not entirely sure if they are. Some things he said match information I know, and other things he said don't match exactly."

"Just tell me what you're trying to say." It was clear Bacillus was growing impatient.

"Yes, Master," Fidus debated where to begin. "Well, one of the most recent things he has said is that apprentices in Atlantis train differently than apprentices here."

When Fidus did not continue, Bacillus looked up at him. "And?" he asked irritably.

"Well, is, uh, I wanted to know if it was true," Fidus answered. He had almost asked a question but had caught himself just in time. He had to remind himself that only Bacillus and a handful of others were technically allowed to ask questions.

Bacillus' expression grew colder, maybe he had detected the question forming, but answered Fidus. "Yes, apprentices are trained differently in Atlantis. They are treated with respect they never earned or deserve from the time they start. They are also given their staffs when they graduate, not when they first begin."

"Yes, the Kale said that was because they had to earn it," Fidus brought up. "I was thinking that was a good idea we might want to use."

"No, Apprentice, it is a terrible idea and untrue. They are forced to work for something that is rightfully theirs, as a sort of motivation to complete their training. We give our new apprentices their staffs right away because our motivation is the conquering of Atlantis. If you are not fully trained, you cannot aid in the act of rescuing Atlantis from its tyranny." Bacillus' entire answer was said in such a sarcastic, belittling tone that Fidus almost immediately thought it was a lie. Maybe not the whole thing, but something about Bacillus' statement was not right. Norvus had never spoken with a tone like that, even when upset. It was always encouraging or pleading, but never mean. Then again, Fidus had never tried to get information from him.

"Is that it?" Bacillus had gone back to his paper.

"No, Master. The first time I guarded the Kale he told me to practice magic--"

"Did you?" Bacillus inquired.

"No, I told him I was forbidden to do so," Fidus replied. Bacillus' tone had made Fidus very grateful he had followed the rules.

"Good."

"As I was saying, when I told the Kale I couldn't, he was surprised. It was as if practicing magic at all times was normal, like *not* practicing was unheard of."

"Yes, in the Palace the sorcerer masters worked the apprentices almost to death. It was very fortunate that I was the most powerful apprentice my age or the weaker apprentices I helped would never have survived. Of course, I could have survived even with the smallest bit of strength."

"See, Norvus said you were not the most powerful apprentice of your age," Fidus realized this was a risky thing to say the moment it left his lips.

"You doubt what I say?" Bacillus' voice was low and menacing.

"Uh, no, that's just what the Kale said," Fidus said truthfully. "I wanted to know if there was any truth in that."

"Apprentice, the fact that you are unsure who to believe tells me you doubt me. The Kale has been putting very dangerous ideas into your head."

Something told Fidus that, if he did not lead the conversation down a different path, he would be in serious trouble.

"Then tell me about power and ability. As the most powerful sorcerer to ever live, people look up to you because of that. You are honored because you have more power than others. But you teach us that if we have more power than others, we have to hide it. That we should not be honored. If we are the Equalizers, we should be treated as equals."

If Fidus had not been so caught up in what he was saying, he would have noticed Bacillus' expression begin to grow more dangerous by the second. But Fidus had not been concentrating on anything besides gaining information without asking questions.

"Now if that is not true," Fidus continued, "Then everything you've taught us apprentices has been a lie! Either we are all treated equally, or we aren't."

"You dare doubt me?" Bacillus growled.

"I'm trying to find the truth!"

"I've told you the truth but you refuse to accept it!"

"Because now I know an alternative!" Fidus stated, jumping from his chair. Bacillus was daunting, but Fidus needed answers. "If you had taught us multiple ways, I would be able to detect the truth for myself!"

"You dare question me?"

"How else am I supposed to learn?" Fidus shouted. A chill passed over Fidus as he realized his mistake. He had asked a question. Bacillus slowly rose from his chair.

"Master--"

"You dare question me?" Bacillus hissed. He stepped towards Fidus.

Fidus stepped back, using the chair as a barrier. "I-- I'm sorry."

"You *dare* question me?" Bacillus continued to walk menacingly forward.

Fidus began to step backwards. "I didn't mean--"

"How *dare* you question me!" Bacillus roared. The sudden exclamation nearly made Fidus fall backwards.

"Master please--"

"Do not run from me you cowering wretch."

Fidus continued to step quickly away from Bacillus until his back touched the wall. Bacillus continued slowly forward.

"Master *please* listen. Let me apologize," he pleaded. Bacillus was now only ten feet away.

"No!" Bacillus shouted, "You deliberately rebelled against everything you've been taught. And for what? Were you hoping for a reward by asking *me* a *question?* No," Bacillus spat, his boiling anger reflecting off the fear in Fidus' eyes. "No, you will be punished."

Bacillus threw his hands forward, threatening to engulf Fidus in the fire that shot from his palms. In pure self-defense Fidus threw his arms in front of his face. A raging wall of water rushed between him and the wall of fire, steam enveloping them both. The wall continued to surge between them. Through the rushing water Bacillus was momentarily surprised. His surprise turned into anger as he increased the energy channeled into the fire. Fidus gasped at the heat coming through the shield. Was Bacillus actually trying to kill him? Fidus was in a bad position. He felt Bacillus' energy shift as flames flew over his shield, nearly catching his hair. Fidus pulled the water over his head, swirling the rest of the shield around him until he was encased in a spinning bubble. Fire beat at the shield, scorching the stone around it. Fidus knew he had to get out of there. He thrust his hand towards Bacillus and a thick stream of water hit him in the face. But instead of distracting Bacillus, the attack only made him angrier. The flames increased dramatically, the heat suffocating Fidus. Fidus increased his attack. Shoving both hands forward, Fidus hurtled his whole shield at Bacillus, extinguishing the fire. Fidus spun his hands around and Bacillus was encased in water, spinning like the Kale did. Fidus ran to the window. He turned and faced his master.

Bacillus threw his hands together and Fidus was suddenly jerked forward. Confused, he concentrated harder on the spell around Bacillus. With a start he realized Bacillus was trying to take over Fidus' spell! He peered into the liquid cage he had constructed. Bacillus had stopped spinning. Fidus brought his hands together, visualizing the orb between his hands. Bacillus began spinning. With a quick movement, Fidus released his hold on the spell. The orb exploded, water flung to every corner of the room, Bacillus sprawled out on the floor.

The man slowly stood, facing his apprentice. They were through testing the others' strength. The steam slowly cleared away. The two sorcerers stared into each other's eyes. Bacillus saw determination, Fidus saw hate. Bacillus pulled back his arms, flames already licking the man's fingers. Fidus pulled all the water he could from the ocean behind him into his power. He could almost hear the energy pulsating through the room. Suddenly, something besides the flames caught Fidus' attention. Something was different between Fidus' energy and his masters. Fidus' felt natural, pure. His master's felt almost artificial. There was a small bit that felt real to Fidus, but the rest was very different. Fidus pushed his curiosity away as he felt the power surge. Bacillus threw his hands forward. They had hardly left his palms when Fidus thrust his outstretched arms in front of him. Two tidal waves crashed on either side of Fidus, every drop in his control. The fire was almost entirely overpowered by the foaming spray. Bacillus was thrown down into rapids, water rushing over him. But he did not forget his other spells. With a flick of his wrists the fire disappeared.

The energy shifted. Suddenly huge chunks of the stone floor were wrenched from their place and hurtled at Fidus' head. With a short cry of surprise he summoned horizontal geysers to push them away. He found himself in another battle of endurance. Thinking quickly he jumped to the side, somersaulting away as he released his hold on the geysers. The small boulders exploded against the floor, pelting Fidus with fist sized rocks. One struck his shoulder with such force that he was sure it was broken. He quickly stood to face Bacillus. Bacillus had a dozen boulders the size of his head hovering in the air. Bacillus was hurling the stones when Fidus acted. He extended his fingers on both hands as to stop the rocks in their path when the room exploded with light, the brightest he had ever summoned. Fidus buried his face in his sleeve at the last second.

Bacillus did not. Fidus heard him cry out as the blinding light appeared before his eyes. Fidus instantly returned the light to normal. The rocks had fallen to the floor as Bacillus covered his face. Without hesitation Fidus threw every drop of water he could at his master. Bacillus felt the full force of the ocean as he was pushed to the far wall. His back slammed hard against the stone, water surging around him, keeping him pasted to the wall. With one smooth motion Fidus released the water. The water crashed back to the floor, creating spray and foam. Bacillus fell to the ground with it, making a considerable splash. He slowly pushed himself up, soaked throughout. Fidus looked around, careful not to take his eyes off Bacillus for long.

The room was flooded with about a foot of water. Everywhere he looked was either scorched or soaked. The little wooden chair he always sat in was nowhere to be seen, reduced to ashes and washed away. Bacillus' throne did not fair too much better. The floor was pockmarked where the boulders had been ripped from their place and Bacillus' elaborate desk had been smashed to pieces, the gems scattered to all corners of the room. Bacillus himself matched his surrounding chambers. He was dripping wet, his crown gone, his black hair in tangles. Fidus glanced down at himself. He was startled to find that not a drop of water had landed on him during the duel. The only reason his cloak was wet was because, when he had released his hold on the water, it had crashed around his legs. He suddenly remembered his shoulder. Inspecting it he discovered the rock had torn a hole in his shoulder and scraped it. He gently wiped away the blood. The corner of his sleeve was charred as well as his elbow. The skin underneath was untouched. He turned his eyes back to his masters'.

Bacillus stood by the previous location of his desk.

He looked Fidus in the eyes. "I am very disappointed in you. I thought that maybe, *maybe,* I could make you something great. I see now that you will never amount to my expectations."

In a normal situation, this would have sent Fidus reeling into despair. But right now, all he could feel was anger and betrayal. Bacillus, the man who had told Fidus' mother that her little boy would always be safe the day they took him to apprenticeship had tried to kill him. What else could that have been? Bacillus had mastered every element of magic, at least, that's what Fidus had believed, and had used fire and rocks to punish him. Even if Bacillus had not meant to kill him, he had obviously wanted to injure him beyond repair. But beyond all the anger and fear Fidus was experiencing, he saw clearly. Before him was a dangerous man, possibly even insane, who did not care how much others around him suffered. The look on his face right before he tried turning Fidus into a living torch held no hesitation.

Fidus knew Bacillus would repeat what he had just done without a second thought and at a moment's notice. Fidus had no intention of letting that happen, to him or to anyone else. So when Bacillus had said how disappointed he was, all Fidus said was, "I understand. I am not fit to be your apprentice."

"You will be sent to the dungeons to be punished," Bacillus replied sharply, "You will remain there until you have learned your lesson. If you attempt to escape or fight against your punisher, you will be punished far more severely. You will wait outside my chambers until a guard can escort you. Leave my sight at once."

Fidus obeyed. He slowly backed out of the chamber, not daring to turn his back on Bacillus. Just as he was about to leave, he looked his master dead in the eye. Without even blinking, he moved his hand towards the window. Every drop of water was pushed gently away. Bacillus staggered as the water in his cloak and hair was pulled back into the ocean along with the rest. Fidus even used the water to push some of the rocks back into their place. When the last drop had trickled back into the sea, the room was as dry as it had ever been. Without saying a word Fidus slowly backed out of the room and into the hallway.

Once out of sight, Fidus leaned heavily against the wall. He had maintained his breathing while in the room, but now it came in short quiet gasps. He slid to the floor as his breathing slowed. He began thinking about what had just happened. The most powerful sorcerer had just dueled him and lost, at least, a sorcerer he had *thought* was the most powerful. When Fidus had taken the water out of Bacillus' cloak, one of his sleeves had been pushed back, revealing five crystals bound to his wrists with gold wire. Fidus now understood why the energy had felt different. Bacillus was using crystals to amplify his power.

It was all a lie. Fidus realized. *Every spell he performed, he made us think he was doing it without the aid of crystals to amplify his power. But he was. The man that taught us lying was a terrible crime, has lied to us since the beginning.*

Two sorcerers came down the hall with staffs in hand.

There, as he was being led down the tunnel to the dungeons with a graduated sorcerer on either side, his faith in the Equalizers and his trust for Bacillus was shattered. Just like the orb of light he had hurtled at Norvus on that first day.

The doubt in Fidus' mind had grown until it could no longer be ignored.

Change of Plans

Fidus had discovered where the middle passage that was at the base of the dungeon stairs led. His punishment had been nothing magical, just brutal pain. He had pushed it from his mind as soon as he could. After he had been punished he had been led to a cell and pushed inside, his escorts placing the same spell over the door that was on the Kale's cell. After the guards left, taking the only light with them, Fidus slumped against the bars that were shared with the adjacent cell in total darkness, and felt something warm.

"Well, I didn't think you would be sent down here this quick."

Fidus jumped back. He peered into the darkness. "Norvus?"

"Yes, Fidus. Tell me," Fidus heard the rustling of cloth as Norvus turned to face Fidus. "What did you do to be sent to the dungeons?

Fidus began from the beginning, leaving out no detail. Norvus listened attentively. When Fidus had finished, the Kale asked, "Have you ever done anything like that before?"

Fidus shook his head, realized it was pitch black, and replied, "No. I've never had a reason to."

"Well, if Bacillus believes that I'm the one putting dangerous ideas into your head, as you said, then why were you placed in the cell next to me?"

Fidus considered this. Norvus heard him laugh softly.

"What is it?"

"Bacillus never clarified what cell I was to be put in, and my guards couldn't ask which one. Now that I think about it, this kind of thing happens a lot."

The Kale smiled, even though Fidus could not see him. "I bet Bacillus wouldn't be too happy to know that."

They sat in silence for a while, both lost in thought. Norvus was about to speak when a small spark appeared in Fidus' cell and vanished. Norvus cocked his head and looked for it again. The light flashed around the young sorcerer's fingers and was extinguished.

"What are you doing?" the Kale asked, a smile playing at his lips.

"I'm testing the spell placed on my cell. I know it prevents magic from going through the doorway and bars, but it doesn't seem to stop magic from within the cell."

"To Bacillus it might have seemed an unnecessary precaution. Not many people can create a spell large enough to be dangerous without the aid of a crystal."

The light flared up again, this time staying lit, illuminating Fidus' face. He wore an expression of disappointment. Norvus looked closer. No, not disappointment; betrayal. He must be thinking about the crystals around his master's wrists.

"I know what you're going through," Norvus said softly as Fidus looked away. "The best thing to do at a time like this is to pray."

Fidus turned back to Norvus. "Pray? How can I do that? I don't even know if this Creator you've told me about actually exists."

"I understand your doubts," Norvus said simply. "But He is real. Just pray for clarity and wisdom on how to respond in this situation. If you suddenly understand what you need to do, or how to act, just thank Him. He's more than happy to help."

Fidus still did not look convinced.

"And besides," Norvus said, "you've got nothing to lose. Either you gain understanding, or you don't. And remember, you already don't have understanding. Things can only get better."

Fidus sighed and looked away. After a while he spoke. "I wonder how long until a guard comes.

At that moment a sound echoed from the stairs. Fidus quickly extinguished the light. As the dark abyss enveloped them, Norvus identified the sound. Footsteps.

"They must have sent a guard."

He was soon proved correct. The footsteps grew nearer and a bright light could be seen up the stairway.

A moment later a short man with dark hair came through the doorway, carrying the largest sphere of light either prisoner had ever seen. It looked as if he had stolen the sun and placed it on his staff. The room was suddenly filled with so much light it could have passed for day. The man holding it paraded down the hall as if it were a rug rolled out for a king. Halfway through his journey, he had the light in his control fly around the room, every so often splitting in half, until about two dozen, fist-sized orbs were spiraling around the room. Three swirled around his head, resembling a crown. Norvus was about to complement the man when a lightning flashed before his face. With a cry he covered his face, trying to block out the radiant explosions all around him. He heard mean laughter. A moment later the attacks stopped.

Norvus closed his eyes and silently whispered a request for guidance. The first word that came to mind was 'gossip.' Puzzled, he stored away the information until it could be used.

Cautiously Norvus opened his eyes, blinking several times to erase the stars he still saw. The lights spinning around the room did not help. He glanced at Fidus and discovered he had suffered an equal fate. Suddenly, the lights froze in their place.

Norvus' vision slowly returned to normal. He turned his attention to the man, who stepped forward.

"Allow me to introduce myself," he said, "I am Oribus," he bowed, "Master of light and fire." He waited, still bowed at the waist, obviously waiting for something. When he did not get it, he looked at the prisoners.

"I'm not applauding you," Fidus said flatly.

"Oh, I don't expect you to." Oribus replied in a mocking voice. "After all, no one like you can be expected to do anything they're supposed to."

"And what's that supposed to mean?" Fidus asked.

The man stiffened. "A question. No wonder you're down here."

"You mean Bacillus didn't tell you anything?" the Kale asked.

Oribus did not answer.

"I can tell you right away that Bacillus told him nothing," Fidus stated.

"King Bacillus," Oribus corrected.

Both prisoners ignored him.

"How do you know?" Norvus asked Fidus.

"Well, I've told you before that there are different levels of sorcerers. There are the apprentices, the masters, the masters of masters, and the Master of all Masters who is Bacillus. Oribus here is just a master."

"I see. I am wondering though, do the masters of masters have apprentices?"

"Yes."

"Do they graduate to master of masters?"

"No."

Lights blinked rapidly in front of their faces, most likely an attempt to stop the questioning, but they were dim. Norvus overlooked them.

"So, how do masters become masters of masters?" the Kale asked.

"Only if Bacillus appoints them. There's no other way."

"I demand that this conversation stop!" Oribus shouted, clearly not being able to handle the large number of questions in such a short amount of time. He tried the lights again but Norvus hardly even saw them.

"Why should it?" Fidus asked. The Kale sighed. Now Fidus was trying to annoy the guard.

"You really shouldn't directly disobey your guard that much," Norvus mentioned.

Fidus looked surprised. "You completely ignored my orders at every chance you got. Especially when I told you to stop asking questions."

"Yes, but I had a purpose for each question. You're just annoying him."

"Enough!" Oribus insisted. He turned to Fidus. Stunningly bright light appeared by Fidus' face, but he was somehow able to stare directly at Oribus. After a moment the guard angrily gave up and said, "I don't want you giving this Atlantis sorcerer any more information about our society."

Fidus whispered to the Kale. "Fine, I'll try it your way." To Oribus he said, "I don't see the harm in telling him what he wants to know. He can't use the information in any way."

Norvus caught on. "Yes, there's no way I could give anything I find out to other Atlantis sorcerers. I don't have enough power. You, on the other hand, can tell everything I say to, uh, *King* Bacillus. Who knows? He might reward you somehow."

Oribus considered this, visibly agreeing with the prisoners.

Fidus glanced at Norvus, a question in his eyes.

"That was good," Norvus whispered.

Fidus smiled slightly and turned away, his expression turning blank. He suddenly seemed to be sitting perfectly still, staring off into space. He shifted weight slightly, crossing his arms. As he did however,

Norvus caught a glimpse of his fingers moving. Fidus was casting a spell.

"You have reminded me that I need information on Atlantis," Oribus spoke up after a bit of thinking.

Norvus suddenly remembered the word gossip.

He sighed loudly. "And that reminds me that today is when the ship comes in."

The man was intrigued. "Tell me what ship."

The Kale sighed again. "Oh, you know, one that brings royal family from somewhere far off. Their sailors and servants always have such great stories."

Oribus leaned forward. "Tell me what kinds of stories."

Norvus almost allowed himself a smile. The man was not asking questions. He waved his hand. "Oh just gossip. I really shouldn't listen to it but I just can't help myself. It's usually about the royal family." Norvus never listened to gossip when he could help it. He despised it. But he pretended otherwise. Maybe he could get information out of Oribus without the guard realizing it.

"Tell me one!" he shouted, clearly excited. "It's been at least five years since I've heard anything about anyone besides the Equalizers."

Norvus began to spin an elaborate tale of boring material. After a few stories Oribus interrupted.

"Your story telling is horrible. Completely unentertaining. Then again you're a sorcerer from Atlantis, I shouldn't expect too much from you."

"Like you could do better," Norvus spat.

Oribus did not need any further prompting. He instantly dove into the juiciest dirt he could dig up on everyone he knew. Norvus appeared to be listening eagerly. After a good ten minutes of useless blabbering, the gossip finally began on something that Norvus was truly interested in.

"Oh!" he declared, "Just today I heard that the Oracle in Atlantis spoke!"

"No!" Norvus declared. Truly interested this time.

"Yes! I heard it myself! After Fidus, the ungrateful thing, had been sent to be punished, King Bacillus summoned me to be the guard. He told me that Fidus had momentarily lost his mind and that the only way to cure him was near solitary confinement for a while. Personally I would have ordered him complete solitary confinement for a month at least. Anyway, while he was telling me everything I needed to do and not do, a man who was sent to spy on Atlantis came in and said he had very important news! I was of course instantly sent away, but not before I heard that the news had to do with the Oracle speaking a prophecy, and that the prophecy could be about King Bacillus' plans to take over Atlantis!"

Norvus gave a low whistle. "What are Bacillus' plans?"

"Well, no one knows for sure, certainly not you of course, but rumor has it that it has something to do with water, and it will happen a day or two after the royal banquet!"

"Water?" Fidus asked, suddenly interested. Fidus had not been paying very close attention to the conversation, but it had taken an intriguing turn.

Oribus nodded his head, forgetting to scowl at the question.

Norvus turned to Fidus. "What if that's why you're in the dungeon and not dead. Maybe you're needed in this plan to take over Atlantis. I'd think that after what you did you would be sentenced to death."

"Why? What'd he do?" Oribus asked quickly.

Without batting an eye Norvus said, "He attacked Bacillus."

"I did not!" Fidus exclaimed, appalled at the idea. "He attacked me!"

"All I'm saying is that if you weren't necessary in Bacillus' plans, Bacillus could have made sure you were killed. You're obviously a threat to him now, so why are you still alive and well?"

Oribus was listening intently, no doubt deciding who he would tell this new bit of information to.

Fidus considered the Kale's point. "I see what you mean," he said. He turned around and resumed staring off into space.

"That reminds me," Oribus continued as if he had never stopped. "There was an apprentice just last week that turned on his master..."

Norvus tried his best to keep an interested expression but he did not know how much longer it could last. Who cared that an apprentice did not like another or that a master was not cruel enough. That was their problem.

After a while Oribus started slowing his pace. He cleared his throat a few times. He glanced at the water clock.

"That cannot be the time!" he exclaimed as he walked over to it. "There's no water! I demand to know if you know anything about this!" He turned to the prisoners.

Norvus turned to Fidus. "Do you know why there's no water in the water clock?"

He gasped as realization dawned on him. "So *that's* where I got the water..."

"At least some of it," Norvus remarked, recalling how large the swirling orb he had been encased in was.

Oribus held back from demanding an explanation. Instead he declared he was going back to the Underground Kingdom for the real time. He cleared his throat and added, "and a drink."

He strolled to the stairway leading up from the dungeons and turned around. With a sarcastic smile, he had half the lights fly from their places around the room and zoom up the stairway ahead of him. The rest followed behind. The last light shot up the stairs and the dungeons were shrouded in darkness. Norvus blinked several times. The dark felt blacker after so much light.

"Did you notice the lights around our faces got dimmer?" Norvus asked Fidus.

"Yeah," Fidus replied. "I'm the one who caused that."

Norvus cocked his head, amused. "How?"

"Well," Fidus began. "I was thinking about my duel with Bacillus. You know how sorcerers tend to gather their spell, to sort of get a better grip on it? Well, if you can pull a spell towards you, you should be able to push it away, right? That's what I did. I have mastered light, remember? It was pretty easy to push away the light. I simply caused the light to not shine in our eyes. Oribus is, of course, not use to having resistance, so he had no idea what was going on."

Norvus chuckled. "Smart. Is that what you were doing with your fingers?"

"I was moving my fingers?"

"Yes, you were."

"Huh. Good to know."

They sat there in silence, each wrapped up in his own thoughts.

Norvus laughed. "I still find it funny you used the water in the water clock when you attacked me."

Fidus smiled in agreement, laughing quietly.

"So," Norvus asked. "What's Oribus' story?"

Fidus sighed. "He's been a master almost as long as the Equalizers have existed. He was never an apprentice, he trained under a master of masters for a while and then graduated. He's had three apprentices in that time, none graduating under him. I was one of them, in the very beginning. I only lasted a week though. All of us were given to another master. The other sorcerers say that we apprentices were just slow, but I honestly believe Oribus didn't train us very well. It's something about his sarcastic, gossipy nature. Did you notice he only lost his sarcasm when he was babbling about other people?"

"Yes, I did."

"Or maybe he just didn't want to teach. I know one of his apprentices said he just had no desire to learn."

"Now hold on. What you've told me of Bacillus makes me believe his attitude is no better."

Fidus shrugged. "It's not, just different. I don't know, something in me wanted to impress him. I found out that could never be done though. Oribus on the other hand..."

Light flew through the room, blinding the prisoners.

"That was fast," Fidus grumbled. "I really don't like that man."

"Hello again, my poor, weak prisoners." Oribus once again paraded down the room, this time carrying a bucket and plate, his staff tucked under his arm. He walked over to the water clock and filled it, carefully setting the time to its correct place. He set the bucket on the floor and sat down next to it, setting the plate on his lap. On it was fresh bread, three slabs of seasoned fish, and a slice of melon. Fidus' eyes, now accustom to the light, grew wide.

"Fruit? Where did *that* come from?"

Oribus took a large bite of the melon, letting the juice drip down his chin. He swallowed before answering. "Unlike you apprentices, we masters get fruit weekly."

"Weekly?" Norvus asked. "How often do apprentices get fruit?"

Fidus sighed. "Only twice a month. Masters of masters get it twice a week and Bacillus gets it whenever he wants."

"The Equalizers huh? Doesn't sound very equal to me." Norvus remarked.

"It is fair!" Oribus retorted. "Everyone in the same class gets the same amount."

Fidus' stomach growled loudly.

"Whoa," Norvus said. "When's the last time you ate?"

Fidus shook his head. "I honestly don't know."

"Well," Oribus said. "You can't have any of mine. If King Bacillus doesn't think you're worthy of having any food, then you won't get any food." He stared down at his plate. "It's too bad," he said sarcastically. "It's *so* good. Why, this fish is seasoned to perfection. And this bread was just baked. I saw it pulled out of the oven. And I can't even describe how sweet and juicy this melon is. It's really too bad you can't have any. In fact, you might not get any as long as you're here in the dungeons. And that is going to be a very long time."

The light suddenly went out. Oribus cried out in confusion. Norvus heard something from Fidus' cell. Suddenly Norvus heard a hollow smack followed by a dull thud and a groan. He peered into the darkness. The light suddenly came on.

Oribus lay on the floor unconscious. Fidus stood behind him, the water bucket in his hand.

Norvus' eyes grew wide.

Fidus spoke before Norvus had the chance. "Change of plans. We're going to Atlantis."

Discussions

"That was a lot of information," Nicky stated as she bit into a loaf of bread.

"Way more than I thought possible," Philo replied.

After they had purchased four loafs of bread for their mid-meal, two sticks of charcoal, and a few blank scrolls, and a bag to carry it all in, the two friends had sat down at a table set up in the marketplace.

"I don't think that we can get all the possible outcomes of this prophecy written down," Nicky stated, looking at the scrolls. "I mean, Teneo's entire room was filled with writings, and not just on the walls and floor. Did you see that bookshelf? It was full of scrolls and papers!"

"He's been working on this for over half a decade. Some of the things written down had to do with events that have come and passed," Philo brought up, "There was a list on the wall with the number three next to it, '*Much will crash without sound, and some will fall yet hit no ground*' remember? Well, one of the things on that list was the island flooding. And that happened four years ago."

Nicky recalled staying in the Palace for almost a month, not wanting to go swimming the moment she walked outside. The sorcerers had to help dry out everything when the water finally receded. She also remembered asking why the sorcerers could not just dry up all the water themselves or, better yet, push it all back into the ocean. She had been told that the water was too powerful and would just flood the island again.

"But if something fell into the water it would make a splash," Nicky countered.

"But if it fell it would hit water, not ground. At least, not right away," Philo argued. "I'm just saying, some of his theories are less probable than others. We could write down the ones we think most likely."

"The island could always flood again," Nicky continued to argue. "We should write down everything."

"But you just said we couldn't get everything written down!" Philo shot back.

"Yeah, well..."

Philo shook his head. "It's been over twenty minutes. Are you done eating?"

Nicky nodded, brushing crumbs off the table. They scooped up the scrolls and charcoal sticks, and headed back to Teneo's house. When they got there, Rachel let them into Teneo's room and they continued analyzing the prophecy.

"Let's continue with line four," Philo suggested.

"*From this disaster will come a tale, one handed down without a fail,*" Nicky read.

Teneo studied a group of words written below the window. "This particular line might not mean anything specific," he began, "but if it did I would guess that mostly storytellers or scribes were left after the disaster."

"Why mostly them?" Nicky asked.

"Storytellers are gifted with good memory," Philo spoke up. "If the tale was handed down without a fail, it means every generation told the next."

"That's right," Teneo confirmed. "Scribes would also be people who pass stories down to the next generation by writing."

Nicky understood and began taking notes.

When Teneo didn't continue, Philo looked to the next line.

"What about line five?" he asked. "*Although life will seem to disappear, Atlantis subjects will still be here.*"

"The sorcerers might turn everyone invisible," Teneo answered.

Philo looked surprised. "Has anything like that happened before? Can people really be turned invisible?"

Nicky turned to Philo. "Lots of things are possible with magic. Being turned invisible isn't that farfetched, is it?"

"Nicky, the sorcerers have figured out that light makes us see things. I don't know exactly how, but if it's light out, you see. But if it's dark, you can't. That's the only way invisibility is possible as far as I know."

"So, maybe something happens that makes it night all the time," Nicky replied. "What if that's what happens if the sun falls!"

Philo nodded grimly. "That does seem to support that theory." He turned to Teneo. "Any other theories on line five?"

Teneo nodded. "Yes. We all die and become ghosts."

The young adults' eyes grew wide. "Die?"

"Yes. Atlantis might be conquered and completely wiped out. After that, all our spirits might continue living here."

Philo turned to Nicky. "It does kind of make sense."

Nicky shivered. "It's too creepy. Can we move on to line six?"

Philo wrote down everything on line five.

Teneo recited from memory, *"The city will crumble yet not decay, if the sorcerers can find a way."*

"The word decay might refer to everyone being dead--" Philo started.

"No! Stop, I don't want to talk about ghosts anymore," Nicky interrupted. She shivered. Things like that scared her.

Philo shrugged and kept writing.

"The city crumbling seems to support the idea of an earthquake," Teneo stated. "Or, maybe the volcano explodes and covers the entire island with volcanic ash. The sorcerers might bring everything back to life, based on *'not decay, if the sorcerers can find a way.'* Or, maybe, the prophecy will come around at a time where the city is built with a type of metal. The island might flood and start to make the metal rust. Over time it would destroy the metal."

Philo kept writing.

"Wait a minute," Philo said suddenly, the charcoal pausing in mid-sentence. "That said *city.* Atlantis is a kingdom."

"Well..." Nicky started. "Compared to other kingdoms ours is on the small side. A few years ago I overheard one of my relatives saying even the smallest city in his kingdom was bigger than the whole island. He may have been over exaggerating though."

"Or Atlantis crumbles, and by the time the prophecy is complete Atlantis is only a city," Teneo spoke up.

"Or it could mean just the villages," Nicky continued. "We've considered the villages a city before."

Philo wrote all three interpretations down.

"What about line seven?" Nicky asked. "*All will lie on them to mend, assisted by enemy that is now friend.*"

"'All will lie on them' might refer to the sorcerers," Teneo said. "It could also refer to the enemy that is now friend."

"So enemy is plural?"

"It could be," Teneo nodded.

"Okay, so who do we know that is our enemy that could assist us?" Philo asked.

Teneo walked over to a list by the door. "Well, it depends on who the enemy that had once been friend is. If the friend that turns on us are horses, the enemy that helps us might be wild dogs. They could chase away the horses before too much damage is done. Another outcome would be if a friendly nation turned and invaded us, an enemy nation might invade them, causing them to pull their soldiers away to defend their home land. That would allow the sorcerers time to form a strategy and protect Atlantis. Or maybe a friendly nation comes to visit our island and they bring a new disease with them. That could conquer our island faster than almost anything else. The enemy nation might have a cure. Or maybe the enemy that helps us is the sickness itself. It might be the key to understanding illnesses."

"Interesting..." Philo mused as he scribbled down the information on the scroll. "Now, what if the enemy and friend are the same, like the illness?"

Teneo walked to another list. "The sun could fall, then rise again, possibly with aid from the sorcerers."

"Or what if the sun falls and it contains something valuable?" Nicky asked. "Maybe multiple things attack us, like the sun falling and a friendly nation. We could maybe bargain with the attacking nation, the sun for a peace treaty."

"That's an interesting thought," Philo murmured as both he and Teneo wrote it down.

"Or what if a sorcerer accidently knocks the sun out of the sky? He would be considered an enemy by removing the sun. He could then find a way to put it back."

"Or," Philo added, "maybe a sorcerer knocks the sun out of the sky because it contains something valuable? What if a sorcerer from long ago hid something in the sun and placed spells around it to keep it safe?"

Nicky gasped, "That could be why it gets colder the closer you get! A freezing spell!"

"Interesting, interesting," Teneo copied it all onto a list.

Philo whistled. "There are just so many possibilities..."

"It's certainly a lot to think about," Nicky agreed.

"That is all I know of the prophecy," Teneo said.

"Thank you so much for your help," Nicky said gratefully.

"And thank you for giving me new things to ponder," Teneo replied.

Philo looked around, copying pictures and lists, just in case they missed anything.

They said goodbye to Teneo, thanking him again, walked downstairs to thank Rachel and say goodbye to her, and left.

"Well, where to?" Philo asked.

Nicky sighed. "I don't know. I think we still need to discuss the possible outcomes and try to figure out which one will happen, if any happen this year."

"Well then, why don't we head over to the Trune's realm? That way no one will know if anyone is eavesdropping. And it's also easier to think away from the villages."

"Good idea," Nicky agreed.

They turned and headed to the Trune's realm.

The Doorway to Light

Fidus and Norvus crept up the stairs, careful to make as little sound as possible.

"So," Norvus asked quietly about half way up the stairs. "What exactly happened down there?"

"Well," Fidus whispered. "I remembered how Bacillus tried to take a spell out of my power. So I tried to take over the spell that kept people from leaving the cell. It was actually a lot simpler to overpower than I thought. I did that right when Oribus came back with his plate of food. I got sick of hearing him brag so I took over his light spell." He turned back and smiled at Norvus, who chuckled in return.

"Just think, a few days ago you didn't even have the courage to ask a question."

"Well, a lot's happened since then."

They reached the door and Fidus extinguished the light. He cracked the door open ever so slightly. The guard was there. Fidus looked around and his eyes landed on the guard's staff. He was about to reach for it, so he could knock out the guard, when another sorcerer walked up.

Great, Fidus groaned, *just my luck they choose now to relieve the guard.* He closed the door silently and motioned Norvus to step back. When they had walked a safe distance from the door, Fidus explained.

"They're relieving the guard up there. And it just so happens that the two sorcerers know each other."

Norvus shrugged. "So, what's the problem?"

"Those two could talk for ages. Every moment they're together they're talking. So we've got two graduated sorcerers to deal with."

Norvus shrugged again. "Just surprise them. You're good at that."

They inched up the stairs and Fidus eased the door open again. The two were standing, chatting about something unimportant.

Fidus spread out his fingers, warmth spreading to his palm. A ball of light flared up between the guards and then rapidly vanished. Both jumped back, blinking rapidly, as Fidus jumped out and grabbed the staff. With it he knocked one on the head, spun around, and slammed the other guard into the wall. Both guards fell to the ground, unconscious.

Norvus came through the doorway. "We should probably hide these two in case someone comes along."

They pulled the two unconscious sorcerers down a few stairs and shut the door. Norvus looked down and noticed a staff.

"Oh! This is useful." He bent down and grabbed it, turning it over in his hands. He threw it lightly into the air and caught it, testing the weight. He laughed triumphantly, but quietly, and turned to Fidus. "Now I will be able to participate!"

They set off in a silent run down the hall.

"I just realized I have no idea what spells you've mastered," Fidus stated, turning to the Kale.

"It's never come up, has it? I've mastered energy." At Fidus' confused look he added, "Not many people study it. I can add or take away energy from any spell. I've also tried some growth magic, which is used mainly in plant spells. To make something grow rapidly, however, you need to supply it with everything it would need to grow naturally. That's why it's so rare to find a sorcerer who's mastered plant spells."

Fidus smiled in spite of himself. Here they were, escaping to Atlantis, and Norvus was giving a lesson on element magic. Fidus suddenly held up his hand and stopped.

"Whoa, hold on," he said, pointing to the rune above the doorway. He started to say the proper incantation, changed his mind, and overpowered the spell. Something that resembled dust exploded down the whole length of the doorway, and floated to the ground. They ran through without a problem.

"Good idea," Norvus said. "Just disable the spells."

A shout rang down the hall, sending shivers down Fidus' spine. He heard more shouts and orders being yelled out. They had been discovered. The two escapees took off down the hallway.

"Do you know where we're going?" Norvus asked, no longer bothering to whisper.

"Of course I do! I've lived here for five years. There's a way up to Atlantis not too far from here." As he said this, three sorcerers, each with staffs, came running from around the corner ahead of them. Fidus did not stop. With a quick gesture a wave splashed down the hall and washed the sorcerers away. They continued running until they came to a fork in the road. There was more shouting up ahead to the left.

"Great..." Fidus muttered to himself.

"What?"

"There are more sorcerers up ahead and that's the way we need to go."

"Well then, make them think we went another way."

Fidus looked around. There were two tunnels behind them and the fork in front of them. He quickly pulled Norvus down one of the tunnels, forming a sphere of light as he did.

"Stay here," he muttered to Norvus.

He then walked to the other tunnel. Once in the tunnel, Fidus looked back. The moment the Equalizers came around the corner, Fidus ran, making sure they saw him. One let out a yell and they all chased him. As soon as Fidus had left the Equalizers' sight, he hid in an adjoining tunnel but kept the ball of light traveling in the same direction. When the sorcerers got there, the light had gone around a corner. They followed it, passing Fidus as they did. When they had gone a safe distance Fidus returned to the Kale and both ran.

For a few minutes the only sounds they heard were their sandals smacking the ground. Then a deafening roar reached their ears. A few moments later a tiger bounded down the hall. Fidus reached for the ocean, having light explode before the tiger's eyes. It turned away but kept running. Water raced down the hall from behind Fidus and Norvus. Keeping his concentration, Fidus had the water rush around them and slam into the tiger. It growled and transformed into a sorcerer. The moment he could, the Equalizer slammed his staff to the ground. Cracks shot through the ground from the staff. The water poured into them. Fidus pushed the water faster, sweeping the sorcerer and the other five that had run up behind him away. He pushed the water away, leaving the floor dry enough to run on without slipping. A ball of fire sped by Fidus' head, nearly catching his hair. The two escapees spun around.

"We should have watched our backs," Norvus muttered. He stepped forward, pressing the end of his staff on the ground. Fidus' eyes grew wide as the moss on the walls grew rapidly, filling the tunnel with a solid wall of greenery. A sorcerer hurtled a few fire balls at it but Fidus doused the flames before they could do any damage.

"I'm getting everything the new moss needs to grow from the moss behind us," Norvus explained. Sure enough, as Fidus watched the moss behind them was rapidly dying. With one last push of energy, Norvus ran down the hall. Fidus followed, soaking the wall of moss for good measure.

They ran up the tunnels, Fidus leading the way and Norvus creating moss walls every couple dozen feet.

As they neared a turn in the tunnel, Fidus slowed considerably.

"What is it?" Norvus asked.

"To get to the exit into Atlantis we need to cross through a main intersection," he said softly. "There are around ten tunnels that branch off of it. It's a perfect ambush point."

Norvus nodded in understanding. "Has anyone taught you to sense when crystals are present?"

Fidus' confused look was answer enough.

Norvus sighed. "It's kind of complicated, it will have to wait." As they neared the entrance to the intersection Norvus closed his eyes. The red gem in the staff glowed softly. Fidus peered around the corner. Not a person in sight.

Norvus opened his eyes. "Crystal sensing is not my strong point, I can't pinpoint anyone." He followed Fidus' gaze into the large room before them. The room was circular shaped, about ten tunnels jetting off into different directions.

"Which one are we aiming for?"

Fidus pointed ahead, slightly to the left. He inched forward, trying to see into the other tunnels. One drawback about the room being lit by phosphorescent moss was that it was impossible to see very far ahead. He inched into the room, listening for anything suspicious. After a few more steps, he bolted for the exit tunnel, Norvus right behind him. The room suddenly exploded with light, causing both prisoners to shield their eyes. Fidus waved his hand and the light around their eyes dimmed, slowly brightening to match the rest of the room. Fidus looked around. A sorcerer stood by the entrance to one of the ten tunnels. As he looked around more sorcerers walked into the light, each from a different tunnel until they were completely surrounded.

"See?" Fidus said. "A perfect place for an ambush." He raised his hands.

"Don't do anything!" A sorcerer yelled, his crystal glowing. The other sorcerers followed suit. Fidus lowered his hands. The sorcerers kept their staffs pointed at the two escapees. Fidus and Norvus stood back to back.

"Any ideas?" Norvus whispered.

"You take the ones over there, I'll take the ones over here. Our goal is to get to that tunnel," Fidus whispered back.

Norvus tightened his grip on his staff. "It's been quite a while since my last duel. This is going to be interesting."

Fidus threw his hands forward, water rushing in from seemingly nowhere towards the sorcerers in front of him. Three he caught off guard, the other two however, were ready for him. The sorcerer to his right thrust his staff forward, a blue orb forming at the crystal and shooting towards Fidus. He ducked, the orb crashing into the wall. Fidus pulled his hand close to his chest and watched water exploded behind the Equalizer, knocking him down. The last hurtled four large chunks of rock at Fidus. Fidus pulled the water into a geyser as a shield, the rocks shooting towards the ceiling as they crashed into the current. Something exploded behind him. With a cry he was pushed into his own geyser. He quickly pulled the water beneath his feet into a dense disk he was able to stand on. He glanced at it, unaware he could even do that. Judging by the look on the other sorcerers faces, they were even more surprised than him. With a grin Fidus spread out his arms like a manta ray and water flooded out from beneath his fountain. He pushed the Equalizers away with such force that they fell the moment the water touched them. Fidus made his hand into a fist as he glanced over at Norvus, causing the water to go around him.

Norvus' foes had attacked all at once. He had taken one down with a tangle of moss. Another had tried to open the ground from under him but Norvus added so much energy to the spell that the ground swallowed the Equalizer instead. The other three had fired multiple colored orbs at him, which he blocked with a shield. Norvus bombarded them with green orbs in quick succession, putting up a shield as one came too close. Every orb that crashed into his shield pushed him back only a few inches, while the orbs Norvus threw launched the Equalizers multiple feet. Norvus had smiled in spite of himself. He never got tired of seeing the confused faces of his foes, who not once figured out that Norvus was taking the energy from their projectiles and putting it into his own. Just then water came from behind him and shoved the Equalizers to the ground. Norvus stole a glance behind him. His eyebrows rose as he looked up at Fidus.

"Brace yourself!" Fidus hollered through cupped hands. He sank to the bottom of the water jet, creating a bubble so as to not get caught in the current, and released his hold on the spell.

The water plummeted down from the ten foot ceiling. Norvus threw a shield in front of him to block the water. He added energy to the water, speeding it up as it crashed against the walls and down the tunnels. The water contained so much power that it rose up the walls and created another wave back the way it came. Fidus pushed it back through the tunnels, carrying eight of the ten Equalizers with it. The ninth was still trapped in the floor, water up to his chest, and the tenth was slowly standing. Norvus spun around quickly, sealing off all but two of the exits with moss, the one they needed and one for behind the Equalizer. The sorcerer slowly crept backwards into the open tunnel, then hurtled a jet of water at Fidus. Fidus threw his hands forward, pushing the water away before it hit him. He gasped as the energy drained away from him. He was once again trapped in a fight of endurance. He felt Norvus place his staff on his shoulder. With the extra energy the spell was still only slightly easier to block.

I'll have to divert it, Fidus thought.

With a shout he pushed his arms to the side, the water streaming against the wall. This required a lot less energy. With a look of shock, the Equalizer forced the water back around at Fidus, who in turn pushed it into a different direction. The surging water wound around the room, flying at Fidus then being diverted. Norvus added energy when he could, stealing some from the Equalizer. As the Kale looked around, he saw a liquid rope, loosely looped around the room, constantly moving. He had never seen anything like it before.

In a last desperate attempt to overpower Fidus, the Equalizer caused the stream of water to fly at Fidus' back. Fidus glanced over his shoulder and, at the last second, ducked, sending the stream shooting at the sorcerer. Caught off guard, the man rapidly pushed it to the side. Fidus, still kneeling on the ground, caused an explosion of light to appear in the Equalizer's face. As the man lost concentration, Fidus took over the water spell, launching every last drop of water into the sorcerer. He was shoved down the tunnel faster than a school of minnows swam to escape a shark. Norvus sealed the exit with moss. Fidus was breathing heavily, his hand still outstretched. With a loud breath his hands dropped to his knees.

Norvus was already breathing hard, but gave Fidus as much energy as he could spare. "You've never exerted that much energy before, have you?"

Fidus shook his head, his hands still on his knees. "No," he breathed heavily, "not even close." He gulped a few more breaths before saying, "we need to keep moving."

"Lead the way," Norvus replied. His eyes strayed to the floor. "Look, someone dropped their staff." He bent down and grabbed it, pushing it into Fidus' hands. "This will help you."

Fidus nodded his head in thanks as he looked over the staff. He noticed the crystal. "My staff had a bluish green crystal too. I gave it to a new apprentice when I found I didn't need it."

Norvus looked surprised. "Just because you can manipulate water without a staff does not mean you don't need one for any spell. Were you ever taught about duel magic?"

Fidus nodded.

"Well, if you were taught correctly, then you would know that in order to perform any duel spells you need a crystal."

Fidus shrugged. "Of course we were never taught that," he announced sarcastically. With a groan he walked forward into the tunnel that lead to the exit. Norvus followed, leaning partly on his staff. They walked up the tunnel with no problem. After about five minutes Fidus suddenly dashed into a smaller tunnel branching off from their current one. He soon came out, carrying a basket full of bread. He had already demolished half a loaf, the other half in his other hand. He held out the basket to Norvus who began to eat hungrily. They continued to walk as they ate, glancing down other tunnels as they walked by them, just to be sure no one was waiting to ambush them again. After they had completely devoured the bread, they came to a hallway slightly larger than the one before, packed full with sorcerers.

Fidus and Norvus stopped cold. *That must be at least three quarters of the Equalizers.* Standing before them were apprentices, masters, and masters of masters.

"Norvus, I can't fight them all," Fidus whispered.

The Kale realized this was true the moment it was said. Neither of them had enough energy to fight even eight of them. Norvus suddenly came to a conclusion.

"Do what you did to me," he whispered back.

"How can I trap them all in individual..." Fidus stopped as an idea came to mind. "Alright!" he exclaimed loudly, raising his hands into the air. "Alright, you've got us. There's no way we could fight all of you." He turned his head towards Norvus ever so slightly and whispered, "Give me all the energy you can spare."

Norvus nodded.

As Fidus dropped his hands, water rushed down the tunnel behind the army, filling it to the ceiling, stopping just in front of Fidus. The Equalizers were thrown into shock as the cold water engulfed them. He pushed his hands apart and the water split right down the middle, leaving a dry path straight through. By then most of the Equalizers had regained enough sense to move. They began swimming out of the water. Fidus twisted his hands and currents began in both tubes of water. Instantly they were all sucked back in and spun around in the walls of water, much like Norvus had been when Fidus had attacked him.

"Let's go!" he shouted. Both he and Norvus ran down the path, sorcerers swirling around and bumping into each other on both sides. The moment they were through walls of water Fidus released them. They crashed into each other, water and Equalizers spraying in every direction. The tidal wave came racing down the tunnel towards Fidus and Norvus.

"Brace yourself," Fidus said.

The water crashed into them, Fidus pulling some together into a dense platform, and shot them down the hall. Fidus strained to keep them afloat on the water platform and away from the tunnel walls. The water slowly got shallower. With a gasp Fidus released the spell. They tumbled down the tunnel a few feet before slowing to a stop.

"Where's the exit?" Norvus groaned, rubbing his elbow.

Fidus looked around, panting. "There," he wheezed.

They scrambled to a heavy wooden door. Fidus located the rune above the doorway, said the proper words, and the door opened. Two sorcerers rushed out from the opening and were immediately smacked in the head with Fidus' and Norvus' staffs. As quickly as they could they climbed the stairs. Fidus' breathing sped up, not just from exhaustion, but from excitement. The stairs went up for what seemed like an eternity. When they at last mounted the last few steps, Fidus said the proper spell, the door opened, and sunlight filled the tunnel.

The Meeting

Nicky and Philo sat in the tall grass of the Trune's realm.

"I think we should stop trying to figure out which one's going to happen," Philo yawned. "After all, even Teneo doesn't know which one is the right one."

They had been discussing the multiple outcomes and which one was most likely to happen for the last half hour.

Nicky looked at Philo and yawned with him. "Yeah, but I feel like we should keep going. We need to be prepared in case it happens soon."

"Nicky, we have no way of even knowing the year this is going to happen!"

She sighed. "I know, I know. I just don't like feeling unprepared for something so huge. There has to be a way to get ready."

Philo took the scroll out of the bag and reread the prophecy. A cool breeze, relief from the hot day, blew through Nicky's hair. She tilted her head back slightly and inhaled deeply, breathing in the sweet grass with just a hint of salt from the ocean. As the wind stopped Nicky looked around. Green trees, flowing grass, delicate flowers. The ocean off in the distance, mountains on the other side of the island, the village. The Palace, the people of the village, her father. All of this could be gone in a matter of days or decades. The prophecy may never come to pass. Not knowing what was going to happen to everything she loved and held dear was driving her crazy. She could live for years, maybe even her entire life, just waiting for her world to end. She lowered her head, placing it in her hands. Maybe it would have been better if she had never found out about the prophecy.

Philo knew exactly what she was thinking.

"Hey!" he said as an idea suddenly came into his head. "Maybe there *is* a way to be prepared!" He quickly scanned the scroll. "Here, line six says, '*The city will crumble yet not decay, if the sorcerers can find a way.* It mentions the sorcerers, no one else, so that probably means a spell of some sort will keep the city alive."

Nicky nodded. "That's a good idea." She grabbed the scroll with the various outcomes. She pointed to the first line. "Okay, so what type of spells could be used in case the volcano erupted?"

"It depends on how it erupts," Philo replied. "I don't see any way that the lava could harm us, since the volcano is so far from where people are. But if the lava was a problem then it could be pushed back to not cause any harm."

"What about all the trees around it? Wouldn't they catch fire?"

"Then a few sorcerers would have to bring water up from the ocean to douse the flames."

"Okay," Nicky picked up the charcoal and began writing on the blank scroll. "What if the lava wasn't the problem?"

"I'm thinking the only way the volcano poses a threat is the smoke it creates. It would probably be very thick and cover the sun. It could also come down over the village and suffocate people."

Nicky wrote this down. Philo took the scroll with the various outcomes written in it.

"If a currently friendly nation attacks us the sorcerers already know what to do."

"Right, they're already trained for battle against enemies," Nicky said as she copied down the information. "What about the next line?"

"Let's see... Ah, the quivering sun. So, if the sun falls, a sorcerer could catch it with a spell."

Nicky suddenly exclaimed, "I just had an idea!" What if a sorceress catches it, and she's the one who sees the quivering sun!"

"Hmm," Philo mussed. "That would mean she's part of the royal family, unless the prophecy is about some other family."

Nicky mulled this over as well. "We haven't had a sorcerer in the royal family in decades. People have even said magic isn't even a trait in my family anymore."

"Maybe she marries in," Philo suggested.

"That's a possibility. We're getting off track. Line two right?"

"Yeah, '*His family will meet, all but one, for she will see a quivering sun*'. Hey, what if the sorcerers make all the girls blind?"

Nicky raised her eyebrows.

"No! Hear me out," Philo continued. "The line says *she* will see a quivering sun. We could prevent the prophecy from coming true that way! Besides, it would have other advantages as well."

Nicky's mouth dropped open. "No! We can't prevent the prophecy! That would force it onto someone who was not prepared! And what other advantages are you talking about?"

"Well, let's admit, it would be a lot easier on us guys to marry if the girls couldn't see what we looked like."

"What? That's what you're worried about right now?" She punched his shoulder.

"Hey, you girls are picky that way."

"We are not."

"Uh, yes, you are."

"Fine, not *all* girls care entirely about appearance."

"But there is a percentage that *does*. I'm telling you, it would solve all our problems."

Nicky laughed once. "Ha! Alright Mister, what would you do with a blind wife and five children? You're working, you can't take care of them."

"I'll just have four daughters and a son I teach my trade. Easy!"

Nicky threw the scroll at him, which he caught. "Alright, I'm just joking."

Nicky sighed. "We're getting off track again."

"Okay, which line's next?"

Nicky read through the prophecy. "Well, I can't see any way that a spell would help in lines three and four. How about line six? What other ways could the city crumble besides actually crumbling?"

"Well let's see... Clay can crumble, rock can crumble. Ugh, I'm stuck in the mindset of actual crumbling."

"Then what's another word for crumble? Wait, can we do that?"

Philo shrugged. "Sure, why not? Okay, there's break, disintegrate, deteriorate, collapse, crush—"

"Let's try collapse."

"Alright, structures can collapse, governments can collapse, the money system can collapse. Wait, maybe it's talking about the marketplace!"

"Yes! What could cause our financial system to collapse?" Nicky asked.

"Well, a war for one. Another would be if no one could work or buy anything. Maybe everyone gets trapped? That could cause some serious problems."

"Like the flood! Remember how everyone had to live on their roofs because their houses were flooded? What if something like that happens again?"

"That could be. So then, maybe the spell the sorcerers cast has something to do with moving through water easier."

"What kind of spells would those be?" Nicky asked as she readied the charcoal.

"Well, maybe the sorcerers move a bunch of logs through the streets to act as bridges. Or maybe they place bridges across everyone's roofs and keep water out of their houses somehow."

Nicky quickly wrote everything.

"Wait," Nicky spoke up. "What about Atlantis seemingly disappearing but not really?" She gasped. "What if they have to turn us all into minnows!"

Philo laughed. He was not being mean, but Nicky's expression of horror was very amusing. Besides, he knew the truth. "Nicky, that would be impossible. Do you remember how Corvus turned into a raven that was as tall as a man?"

She nodded.

"He couldn't transform into a normal sized raven because where would the rest of him go?"

Nicky looked confused.

Philo tried again. "Alright, so if someone weighs ten pounds, and then tries to turn into something that weighs three pounds, where do the other seven go? The same thing happens if something three pounds tries to become something five pounds. Where does it get the other two? The two things have to weigh the same. Corvus had to use all of him to transform into a raven, he couldn't get rid of or add anything to himself. Does that make sense?"

Nicky nodded. "So, what if they changed our feet into fish? Or maybe they add fins to our feet?"

"I'd think that you'd fall over," Philo said. "But turning into something that swims might be something that could happen."

Philo shook his head. "Let's stop going through line by line. Let's try just looking at the possible ends of Atlantis. For example, one of the things that conquers Atlantis could be a volcano, which we've already discussed."

"We've already talked a little about the sun falling," Nicky put in.

"Well let's talk about it some more. If the sun fell on its own, the sorcerers could contain it in a spell, keeping everyone safe from its heat, or cold if the freezing spells are real. Another spell could be to put the sun back in its place to keep us from decaying."

Nicky wrote everything on the scroll. "So, the enemy that had once been friend from line one could be the enemy that is now friend from line seven. Right?"

"Yeah, but I don't know how likely that is. I mean, if a nation attacks us I don't know how they would just change their minds and help us."

"What if the sorcerers perform some kind of spell that makes them want to help us?"

"As in, change their minds? I don't think that's possible."

"Hmm... Well what if the sorcerers transformed some of the enemy into animals? That could scare them into helping us if they did it right. Remember, sorcerers are only on Atlantis, nowhere else. Not this kind of magic anyway."

"That's a good point. What would scare them enough to make them agree to help us?"

Nicky considered Philo's question. "What if we get attacked during a flood and the sorcerers have transformed everyone? Then when the nation attacking us sees that everyone has fins instead of hands and feet they might get scared and run away?"

"Hey! What if the enemy in line one are the sorcerers? Maybe no one likes the transformation and get really mad at the sorcerers. Then when someone attacks us, they get scared and run off, then suddenly the sorcerers are our friends again."

"That could actually happen!" She wrote it down.

Philo looked behind Nicky and suddenly stood up. He raced around her, pushing his arms out as if he was protecting her. She stood and spun around, looking over Philo's shoulder. Coming up to them was a thin, slightly pale man somewhere in his early twenties. Possibly younger. His thick black hair came down to just above his neck and he was leaning slightly on a cane as he walked. As the man pushed it forward to take another step, Nicky realized it was a sorcerer's staff. This man was a sorcerer, and Nicky did not know him. Philo stiffened as the man came closer.

"Hey!" The sorcerer called out.

"Who are you?" Philo shot back.

"My name's Fidus. I need to speak with the king immediately."

"What business do you have with the king?" Nicky spoke up.

Fidus looked at her. "I have information about an enemy of his."

Nicky was instantly curious. "What enemy?"

"I don't think I should tell you. Can you please tell me how to get to the king?"

Nicky stood up a little straighter. "I am the princess. My father's enemy is my enemy. Now who is this enemy you're referring to?"

Fidus looked around, as if worried someone was following him, or someone was supposed to be following him and was not.

"Nicky," Philo whispered. "This is a sorcerer who we don't know and that has information of an enemy. He could be a spy trying to trap you."

"Maybe," she whispered back. An idea suddenly came to her mind. To Fidus she said, "Let me rephrase the question. What kind of information do you have of this enemy? His location? His plans on conquering Atlantis? Plans on hurting my father?"

"Yes! All three. Please lead me to the king, this is getting more urgent as we speak.

"Nicky," Philo warned.

"Philo! He said the enemy is planning to take over Atlantis! What if this could be the prophecy?"

"Philo?" Fidus recognized the name, it was clear on his face. Fidus walked closer, studding every inch of Philo's face. Philo backed away, keeping Nicky behind him.

"Philo!" He suddenly exclaimed, straightening up. "You're Dedri and Camena's son!"

Philo stared at the man, distrust evident in his eyes. "How would you know that?"

"Lessus, Camena's sister, is my mother. Philo, you're my cousin!"

"Wha-- no. I've never had a cousin Fidus."

Fidus was determined. "No, you did! I've been gone for five years! Your older brothers, twins, went into glass making seven years ago. I remember your eighth birthday, when you were accepted as a sorcerer's apprentice!"

"I still don't trust you..."

"Philo, is you're scar hurting?" The scar.

This question left Philo shocked. His arms dropped almost to his sides, still subconsciously protecting Nicky.

"What's he talking about?" Nicky asked.

Philo flashed back. He had been practicing duel magic, creating his few first orbs.

"Your scar," Fidus persisted. "I remember when your parents were rushed over to the palace, told there had been an accident."

He had lost control. It exploded in his hands.

"You were in shock. Your hands were almost completely burned."

The pain. The hot, searing pain.

"Philo what on earth is he talking about?"

"The sorcerers were afraid to help, not knowing exactly what you had done."

The grown-ups rushing towards him as he curled into a ball on the floor. The shouting, the spells over his hands. Someone was shaking him. He blinked back to reality. He turned to face Nicky, concern on her face.

"Philo. What is he talking about?" It was more of a statement than a question.

He looked down at the scar on his left hand. It was not very large, mostly the outer edge of his palm and only stretching from the first knuckle of his little finger, to just above his wrist. It was not that noticeable to anyone else, only a shade or two lighter than the rest of his skin.

"I never told anyone about my scar," he said finally.

Desperation was in Fidus' voice. "Philo, *you* never told anyone. The sorcerers told your parents, who told immediate family. That's how I know about it. I was there when you were sent home, when the burns all healed except for your scar. Please believe me. You should know I mean you know harm."

"What does he mean by that?" Nicky almost shouted. She nearly grabbed Philo's hand. "What makes this scar different. Why have you never mentioned it when all the other boys are bragging about their scars?"

"Because it helps me sense danger." His voice was barely above a whisper.

"What?" she stared at him. "Why haven't you told me this? Are you embarrassed or something?"

"No," Philo said. He did not know where to start. He turned to face her, spilling out the words all at once. "After the accident, I didn't want to come back to the palace ever again. But your father asked me to. He said that he didn't want you having to be surrounded by guards whenever you wanted to play. He told me that his father had guards around him at all times. So when your father grew older, he would try to escape from them just for his own amusement. He said he didn't want you doing that, just in case something happened when you were unprotected. We were already friends, so he asked me to look out for you. I never told you because I didn't want you thinking that was the only reason I spent time with you." He braced himself for her reaction, even though he had no idea what it would be.

Understanding filled her face. "It all makes so much more sense now! How you would never step on glass in a room full of it, or how you pushed me out of the way when Corvus tried to grab me. I thought it was luck, but I don't believe in luck, so now it all makes sense! I wish you had told me about the accident though. I never knew that's why you quit being an apprentice."

He sighed. They were still friends. Suddenly they heard a feeble shout. The three spun their heads in the direction it came from. Another sorcerer was walking up the hill, this one leaning heavily on his staff.

"Fidus!" He said when he came closer. "Where did you go?" His eyes strayed to Philo and Nicky. "Princess!"

"Kale Norvus! You're alive!" She came very close to running out and hugging him. She might have if Philo had not flinched.

"Something's happening," he said.

Nicky gasped. "The prophecy?"

Norvus looked around, as if for an answer. "The prophecy? What prophecy?"

"Princess, can I *please* speak with your father?" Fidus implored again.

Nicky looked at the three faces. She quickly stuffed all the scrolls into the bag. "Let's go."

Philo rubbed his left hand. "I think we should hurry."

Forced into Action

"What do you mean he escaped?" Bacillus thundered as the sorcerer before him trembled.

"Exactly that, Sire," the master stuttered, not even looking at Bacillus. "Both prisoners have fled the dungeons and are now in Atlantis."

Bacillus drew back his arm, flames already igniting around his fingers. The master recoiled, clenching his eyes shut. Bacillus abruptly turned away, letting the flames dissolve.

This cowardly Equalizer was a master of wind, one of the best, and was needed for the plan to work. *I'll punish him later,* Bacillus reasoned, *but for now he must live.* He studied his chambers with loathing. The room was bare, all the furniture having been burnt during his duel with Fidus. He scowled at the mere thought of the apprentice's name. After all he had planned, after all his precautions, Fidus had still turned on him. He had let down his guard, had too much faith in his plans. The one time he had followed his advisors advice, putting Fidus in charge of the Kale, had led to this near disaster. He made a note to destroy the advisors as well. He looked around at the scorched floors and walls, slowly being washed clean by apprentices. His hate-filled eyes slid to the ocean, held back by the window.

"Sire?"

He spun around. "What?" he spat, his arm raised to punish the question. Next to the master stood Volcanis, a master of masters, an Equalizer allowed to ask questions. Bacillus lowered his arm but did not relax.

The master of masters flinched but stood his ground. "Sire, what do you propose we do?"

"We have no choice. We attack Atlantis now."

The man was visibly shocked. "B-but Sire—"

"Right now a traitor is on his way to the Palace, guided by an Atlantian sorcerer!" Bacillus shouted venomously. "We cannot risk him announcing our location or anything about us to the Atlantian King!"

"What are you saying?"

He looked the two sorcerers in the eyes. "Fidus is now considered an enemy, so he will be destroyed like one. We will attack Atlantis with everything we have. We act, and we act now."

Volcanis looked him in the eyes. "I'll call the Equalizers." He bowed then ran from the room. A few moments later a gong echoed through the tunnels. Once. Twice. Three times.

Bacillus took his staff and marched out of his chambers. On any other day he would not have needed his staff, he had enough crystals around his wrists to perform any spell, but today he needed every crystal he could get. He was not far from his destination, the western most part of the Underground Kingdom. He was one of the first to arrive. He looked around the circular room. Three tunnels branched off of it at one end. Opposite the tunnels was a window holding back the ocean. Light flowed through the water and danced over the walls and floor. Bacillus positioned himself in front of the window, his back to it. His followers quickly filled the room. A large group came in all at once, every last one dripping wet.

"Why are you all so wet?" Bacillus demanded. The group looked up with apprehension. One stepped forward.

"Sire," he bowed. "We were attacked by..." he glanced up tentatively. "By Fidus."

Bacillus gave out an exaggerated sigh. "Yes, my former apprentice."

Volcanis whispered to Bacillus, "Everyone is present."

Bacillus summoned part of the wall. With a crack it flew towards him. He stepped up on it to address the crowd.

"My loyal followers, my equals," he began. "Today I bring both good news and bad news. I am pained to say it, but my apprentice Fidus has been brainwashed into leaving the Equalizers and everything we stand for to go to Atlantis." Bacillus let the gasps of dismay and shouts of anger die down before continuing. "Yes, I'm afraid it's true. Once I discovered his disloyalty I sent him to the dungeons. I knew that there was hope for him but I couldn't attend to him right away. Unfortunately he escaped before I could straighten out his thoughts. But do not lose heart! This terrible thing will lead us to glory! By running off to join Atlantis' sorcerers he has given us the perfect opportunity to act! Yes, my friends, we will take Atlantis today!"

Cheering rose up from the crowd.

Volcanis turned his back to the crowd and leaned close to Bacillus. "Sire, we cannot attack using the original plan. The tides are wrong."

"I don't care," Bacillus hissed back threateningly. "Fidus is a threat to the overall plan. We cannot wait any longer."

"Sire, even if the tides were not an issue, Fidus was still a vital part of this plan. Without him we lack fine water control."

"Find someone else then!"

"It's not that simple. Sire I do not see this plan unfolding the way you want. It may be better if we have one of our spies eliminate Fidus quietly—"

"Do you forget who makes the decisions?" Bacillus looked him in the eye, daring him to question his king.

Volcanis backed down. "No, Sire. Of course not. Tell me what you need done."

"That's better." He straightened to address the crowd. "Everyone listen. Anyone who has mastered water come forward. Masters of wind follow." The Equalizers did as they were told.

"What we're going to do, is summon a wave large enough to cover the entire Palace from the west, right up the Trune's Bay. When the wave reaches the Palace, the masters of wind will help the masters of water form a cyclone around it, forcing it through every hall and into every room. Once the entire royal family has drowned, you will release the water spell. This will allow us to eliminate the royal family without destroying Atlantis. When that task is complete, I will give the rest of the instructions. Act now."

The masters of water lowered their staffs so that the crystals were touching, to focus the power. The masters of wind did the same, aiding the masters of water. The room began to glow, murmuring was heard. Bacillus looked out at the ocean. The water slowly pulled away. He allowed himself a smile. In a few short hours he would be king of Atlantis.

***

Nicky and Philo ran as fast as they could. Philo had asked the two sorcerers if they could fly to the Palace, like the Trune did, but they did not have enough energy. Nor could they create a disturbance large enough to attract the Trune's attention. So the younger two ran while the sorcerers walked as fast as they could.

Nicky and Philo ran through the Palace gate and up the marble staircase. They turned left into a small room. In the very middle was a thick rope, surrounded with twelve smaller ropes. Each of the smaller ones had sorcerer's title next to it. Nicky ran right to the middle and pulled it twice with all her might. The entire rope began to glisten a light purple, starting from where it disappeared into the ceiling. After a minute, the rope returned to its natural white and Nicky ran to the sorcerers' conference room. Within seconds of her getting there most the sorcerers appeared around her, walking through magical doorways.

"Princess! What's happened?"

"Why have you summoned us?"

"What's wrong?"

At that moment the last sorcerer appeared, bringing King Neptus with him.

"Nicky!"

"Here is what's going on," Nicky declared. "The prophecy is happening, and we need to be prepared."

The room exploded with exclamations of distress and anger.

"Alright silence. Silence!" King Neptus yelled, raising his hands. The twelve sorcerers held their tongues. "Nicky, how could you possibly know? Do you have any proof?"

At that moment the doors burst open. Four armed guards and eight sorcerer elders walked through the doorway in a tight cluster. They separated slightly as they entered the room, revealing Fidus and Kale Norvus, whose staffs had been confiscated. Nicky noticed with dismay that two of the guards had a tight hold on both of Fidus' arms. The twelve sorcerers around her instantly held their staffs up, ready for trouble.

"No, we can trust them!" Philo spoke up for the first time.

"We don't know that, Philo," the King spoke up. He approached the two prisoners. A sudden but slight look of surprise crossed his face as he recognized Norvus. "Kale Norvus—"

"Your Highness," Norvus said suddenly. "Please forgive me for interrupting, but I personally vouch for

Fidus here. He helped me escape from our enemy and risked his safety multiple times to save mine."

"That may be true, but we still have a procedure," Neptus replied.

"Your Highness, there's no time," Fidus said bluntly. He grimaced as the guards tightened their hold. He took a breath and began. "As we speak Bacillus is planning to conquer Atlantis." A small murmur arouse at the mention of Bacillus. Fidus continued. "Over the years he has collected people gifted with magic and taught them to hate Atlantis and its people. He trained us to be his army. For the last five years I have trained under him as an apprentice in the underground volcanic tunnels. Years ago Bacillus and his early followers emptied out all of the lava and water." Four of the eight elder sorcerers lowered their staffs to his face.

"Why are you telling us this?" the King asked.

"Because I've seen what he's capable of and I had to warn you. He preaches equality and fairness but twists their true meaning. He is planning to take over Atlantis and make it his own, and frankly I believe he could do it."

"Is he talking about *the* Bacillus?" Mur Alana asked.

Norvus nodded.

Bos Trenious stepped forward. "Alright, let's say we believe everything you've just said. If Bacillus is so powerful, how did you even get here? Wouldn't he have stopped you, since you're telling us information he would probably want kept secret?"

Fidus shook his head. "We escaped. The way he has set up his kingdom has a lot of drawbacks. He doesn't get all the information he needs at the time he needs it, thankfully for us."

"That still doesn't answer my question."

Norvus spoke up. "We were able to escape because we had surprise on our hands. No one knew how powerful Fidus is, none of them stood a chance. Why do you think we're so exhausted? We didn't just walk away. We had to fight, and we barely made it out."

"How can we know that this isn't just a distraction of some kind?"

Philo blurted out, "Because my scar is hurting." He walked up to the twelve sorcerers, holding his hand. "Do any of you remember when I was an apprentice here?"

Recognition fluttered across their faces.

"I can sense danger. I know for a fact that, as of right now, we are not in danger, but we will be very soon. You have to trust us, or at least hear us out," Philo pleaded.

"Alright," Cor Ambris said. She turned to Fidus. "What is Bacillus planning?"

"I-- I don't know for sure."

"Well then what are you here for?" Bos Trenious declared impatiently.

"I'm here because I know that Bacillus is planning *something*! You can't have expected him to tell me everything, or anything for that manner. I was just his apprentice, someone for him to discourage and manipulate."

"Well, do you have *any* information besides guesses and accusations?"

There was momentary silence.

"We know that he might be planning something with fire," Norvus spoke up.

"How?" Fidus asked, "Oribus said that he was planning something with water."

"Fidus, think," Norvus responded, acting as if it was just them talking, not surrounded by distrusting guards. "Look at how many people down there have mastered fire. If Bacillus is truly training an army to conquer Atlantis, then wouldn't he demand that they learn specific things?"

Something clicked in Fidus' mind. "You're right. Come to think of it, there were only four main elements that apprentices were taught to manipulate. Fire, wind, water and stone."

"Great!" Nicky exclaimed, "What could Bacillus do to conquer Atlantis with those?"

Philo grabbed the bag from Nicky, franticly searching through it for the right scroll.

"Here," he announced, unrolling the scroll. "Do you think Bacillus is planning to set off the volcano?"

"How would he even control something that big?" Rus Nevik spoke up.

Philo showed him the scroll. "See?" he pointed to the first line, "These are all possible outcomes of the prophecy. For example, all life seeming to disappear in line five could mean that everyone is turned invisible. Or here, 'the enemy that had once been friend' in line one could be a nation belonging to the royal family or just a friendly nation."

Philo looked up as he realized the sorcerers were staring at him.

"Where did you get that list?" Quen Anrym asked.

Nicky spoke up. "We visited Teneo. He told us what he knew and we were able to add ideas to his lists."

Trune Sapphirell shook her head. "We have a list like that already. You did not need to talk to Teneo."

"I thought you were all mad at me for learning about the prophecy," Nicky said, slightly embarrassed.

King Neptus shook his head. "Regardless of where the information was found, what are we doing with this knowledge?"

"Getting prepared!" Nicky exclaimed.

"Princess," Cor Ambris started. "Unless we know the actual outcome of the prophecy is I don't think we can prepare for it."

"No, see, that's what the list is for!" Nicky jumped over to Philo, pointing to the scroll. She dug through the bag and unrolled the scroll with the prophecy written on it as the Cor walked over.

"Here, we already know that the enemy that conquers us in line one is Bacillus," she began.

"Let me see that," Norvus said, stretching out his arm as he took a step towards her. Three of the sorcerer elders instantly restrained him. Nicky ran over to him and handed him the scroll. He quickly scanned through it, Fidus reading over his shoulder.

Nicky pointed to each line as it was read and kept talking. "And we're pretty sure the family in line two means the royal family, which are all here right now for the banquet. And in line three, the soundless crash could mean the sorcerers put a spell on everyone so that they can't hear anything. And in line four everyone but scribes and story tellers die out, possibly—"

"Nicky!" Neptus said forcefully. "How does this help us get prepared?"

"The sorcerers in line seven! It says '*All will lie on them to mend.*' The only way we can think of that happening, them mending the disaster that follows the prophecy, is if they discuss spells!"

"Alright," Rus Nevik said. "I see the logic behind that. But how can we know for certain that the prophecy is happening now?"

"Because," Fidus spoke up. "I was one of Bacillus' most powerful followers. He knows I'm coming here to warn you... He's going to act now. He has to or he loses the advantage of surprise."

Norvus spoke up. "Please, believe us. I've seen this first hand, he has a quite a few followers, most of whom are graduated sorcerers. At least half of the ones we fought were just as skilled as you or I. And I have very little doubt that he needed Fidus for his plan to work."

"And he's going to want to attack when I'm still exhausted from escaping. I showed him my full power and he won't rest until I'm destroyed. He can't have anyone who knows that they're more powerful than him."

"He's right," Nom Drach said. The other sorcerers turned to look at him. "Do any of you remember when Bacillus was an apprentice here? He always wanted to look the best, so he would try to take out anyone that showed him up." He turned to Fidus. "If you're anywhere near as powerful as you say you are, he's coming for you."

"We need to at least discuss possible spells that could save Atlantis," Trune Sapphirell insisted. "If Fidus here is lying, then we wait until next year for the prophecy. If he's telling the truth, then we could save a lot more people."

"Alright," Bos Trenious said finally. "I'll go along with this.

"Great!" Nicky nearly sighed with relief. Philo handed her the scroll and she took it. "Okay, so possible ends to Atlantis are the volcano, the sun falling, a flood, a stampede of horses—"

"A flood," Fidus repeated barely audible.

"--an attack by another nation, enemy sorcerers—"

"A flood! That could be it!" Fidus exclaimed.

Philo raised his head. "Why does a flood stand out?" He asked.

"As I said earlier, Bacillus followers the Equalizers have all mastered manipulation of fire, wind, water, or stone. Those who have mastered water could push it onto land, with the help of those who have mastered wind."

Philo suddenly clutched his hand, the scroll falling to the floor. No one noticed.

"What about the fire and stone?" Tem Prisidious asked.

"Uh, fire could be used to dry up the water, turn it to steam. Maybe the masters of water will have to hold the spell so long that, after they release it, they're too exhausted to push it back into the ocean."

Philo took a sharp breath. Nicky heard it. "Philo, what's wrong?"

"Alright, let's go along with the flood theory," the Rus spoke up. "What kind of spells could be used to aid the people of Atlantis?"

Mur Alana reached into the bag that Nicky had placed on the floor. "Here's a scroll of possible spells. According to this we could turn everyone into fish..."

"It could work," Norvus spoke up.

"I-- I don't know," Philo whispered to Nicky. "My scar's never felt this way before." He gave a small gasp and held his hand tighter.

"Do you think it's the prophecy?" Nicky whispered back. Philo could only nod, his eyes large with worry and pain.

"What if Bacillus is planning to set fire to everything," Quen Anrym brought up. "It would make more sense that the water was to douse the flames, and the wind was to make them bigger."

"That could be it. Mur Alana, is there anything about fire in that scroll?"

She shook her head.

"Maybe we could create a spell that makes it impossible for everything in Atlantis to burn."

Mur Alana took the charcoal and wrote it down.

Nicky was concerned about Philo. He looked as if he was in serious pain.

"It's not like anything I've felt before," he kept saying. "It's a constant, throbbing pain, unlike the small, quick stabs I would get when I needed to move out of harm's way quickly."

Nicky opened her mouth to say something when she heard a bell. Soft, faint, yet distinct. She walked out of the chambers and up a flight of stairs. Philo followed. At the top of the stairs was a door that led out to a balcony. She quickly opened it and walked out to the railing. The wind was so fierce it almost knocked her to the floor. Struggling against it, she made her way to the railing. Taking hold of it, she looked around. She was standing on a balcony looking out on the Trune's bay. Everything looked normal at first, until Nicky noticed the Trune's entire realm, which was mostly water, was dry. At the edge of the island, just to the left of the bay, was a green and blue flicker. A warning flare. She watched as another flare the same colors sprang up, closer this time and on the right side. She heard another bell tolling. The warning bells.

In case there was ever any danger or they were ever attacked, the people of Atlantis had created a warning system. The lookout that first saw the danger would light the flare and ring a huge bell. Another person in a different place would then see the flare and hear the bell. He would light his flares and also ring his bell. Depending on the type of danger, the lookouts would throw different minerals into the flames, causing the flares to be different colors. Orange stood for a hurricane or strong storm. Blue was water related, either a flood or tidal wave. Purple was if enemy war ships were sighted, and green was for any other danger. It was an effective system that quickly and progressively brought news of danger to everyone on the island. More flares and bells were being set off, spreading through the rest of the island. She looked over to the left at a village and saw people scrambling around, gathering important items and family members.

"It's happening," Philo said.

"Green and blue flares. Unknown and water related." Nicky stated, trying to keep her hair out of her face. Something moved in the distance, just outside the Trune's realm. A dark shape steadily grew out of the ocean. Water suddenly gushed back into the bay. With unsettling speed it rushed into the bay, growing as it did. Nicky leaned closer, trying to get a clear picture of the danger. It rose up until it covered the sun, but instead of blocking its light, it distorted it.

"Nicky, it's a wave!"

Her eyes grew wide as she realize what Philo said was true. Her jaw dropped open as she saw the sun through the water, quivering.

The mountain of water was now halfway to the Palace and almost as tall.

Nicky spun around, running to the sorcerers. "It's a wave!" She shrieked. She ran as fast as she could down the stairs, all the while screaming, "It's a wave! It's a wave!"

The Outcome

The sorcerers bolted through the door, running up to the balcony to see for themselves. Philo was hunched over, leaning against the wall. He had not even made it halfway down the stairs. Nicky ran to him.

"Everyone's in danger," he gasped, his hand clenched over the other. "No one is safe, everyone is in danger."

Fidus ran up to them, no longer being guarded. The sorcerers were all on the balcony, rapidly shouting, asking questions.

"You need to get somewhere safe," Fidus instructed them.

"Fidus!" Rus Nevik yelled over the wind. The apprentice spun his head towards the call. "You said you weren't an Equalizer anymore. Well now's your chance to prove it." Fidus ran to the balcony.

He was slammed against the wall by the wind. "What's going on?" He could instantly tell that this wind was not natural.

"They formed a wave but based on its size I don't see how they'll control it. We need you to keep the water away from the Palace if you can."

A few of the Atlantian Sorcerers had formed a barrier to keep the wind off the balcony. Fidus ducked as a palm tree flew by.

Fidus shook his head. "I have no energy left. How can I stop *that*."

"Do what you can."

"What are you planning to do?"

"Just concentrate on keeping that wave away from us." The sorcerer thrust a staff into Fidus' hands and joined the others. Fidus turned to see Philo and Nicky still on the stairs.

"Run! Get somewhere safe!" He pushed the end of the staff on the ground and braced himself.

Nicky and Philo ran down the stairs and around the corner.

"Nicky, where—"

"There are stairs over here that lead up! Come on, we can make it!" She pulled Philo along as fast as they could go.

The sorcerers, along with the apprentices and elders who had been summoned, stood in three circles on the balcony. The apprentices stood in a circle, the graduated sorcerers stood in a circle around them, and the elders stood in a circle around them. They all had the crystals in their staffs pressed together, to better focus the power of the spell. Fidus stood apart from them, closing his eyes for better concentration.

This is just like the dolphin, he realized. *Just like the air pocket around the dolphin.*

The water was surging closer every second, nearly perfectly controlled by the Equalizers. The unbroken wall of water climbed steadily towards them, accumulating everything left in the Trune's bay. Driftwood, fishing boats, royal ships, anything it could grab. A fisherman's raft was caught in the torrent was propelled up the surface of the wave, long since abandoned by the fishermen. The crest was much higher than the top of the Palace now, quickly coming toward them. A shadow passed over the balcony. Fidus looked up, no longer able to see the top of the wave clearly. The wave was nearly upon them. He lowered his head and concentrated. He had one chance to get this right. Just before it hit the Palace, the wave was stopped by Fidus' spell. The water smashed angrily against the barrier far above them. It broke for a second, sending spray in every direction, but quickly regained form and began swirling around the Palace. Fidus planted his feet firmly to the ground, trying his best to stay standing. His breath was coming in slow gasps. The water continued to spin around the Palace, aided by the wind. Fidus felt more water being added to the attack, hundreds of gallons at a time. Then something happened.

In the Underground Kingdom, the power pulsating through the room was nearly visible. Bacillus watched, adding energy to keep the spell alive. Suddenly he felt the water fighting- not following- their command.

"What's going on?" he demanded. He saw people start to collapse. He faltered as he realized they were losing the spell. "No! More energy! We need to—"

"Sire there-- there is no more," Volcanis gasped.

"Cease all other spells!" Bacillus roared, refusing to let the strain he felt show.

The sorcerers began deactivating other spells. The underground light dimmed as the spell that enhanced light was removed. As more spells were broken Bacillus felt the wave slowly returning to them. Suddenly the window behind him vanished. Thousands of gallons of water rushed through, pounding the Equalizers into the halls around them. Bacillus was pummeled about the caves, along with the other masters. Most were knocked unconscious instantly, others drowned. The water churned, rushing through the tunnels, blasting away the walls. In a desperate attempt to regain control Bacillus thrust out his hands, sending water away from him in every direction. The water flew through the doorways, taking with it chunks of the unstable walls around the entire Underground Kingdom. With all window spells gone, the water was unrelenting in its deviation of the tunnels. The tunnel around Bacillus shook violently and collapsed, crushing Bacillus and the others with him under thousands of pounds of meteor and lava rock. The entire island was suddenly collapsing under its own weight, successfully crushing each layer of tunnels below.

The entire wave shook, and it fell. Fidus nearly collapsed, landing on one knee, as the full weight of the water was pushing against his spell. Norvus glanced up. The water was falling down an invisible dome. He watched it, fascinated. The water surrounded the Palace, held away by a hand's width of air. It was as if the entire Palace was submerged in a glass egg. Norvus tried to peer through the turbulent sea but could not. Fidus was gasping for breath, shaking violently, leaning heavily on the staff.

"Stay strong Fidus!" Norvus shouted. "We're almost there!" The boundless water was raging against Fidus' barrier. Norvus turned his focus back to the other sorcerers, feeling a sudden drain on his energy. He listened to the spell, putting as much energy as he could into it.

"I- I can't--" Fidus was gasping, deathly pale. With one last push of energy, the boy collapsed. The spell around the Palace failed. Water thundered down, crushing the sorcerers beneath its weight, washing them away along with their half completed spell.

The water flung itself into the gardens, uprooting flowers and toppling statues. The ocean flew out the open gates, pushing guards aside like grass. It charged into the villages, taking possessions and people whenever it came across them and moving them wherever it wanted. People yelled and ran but were instantly silenced and overtaken. It smashed into houses, crumbling the clay and reducing the wooden frames to splinters. People scrambled into their houses for safety, only to be thrust against the walls by the wave. Few made it to high ground. The ocean claimed every cart, shop, and trade, discriminating against nothing. It chased a young mother and her child. She grabbed her son as she jumped to a ladder on the side of a shop, climbing rapidly. The water crashed into the wall, welling up around her, soaking her, but not able to grab her. It reared back and was suddenly sucked into the ground. A sinkhole had opened. Another appeared nearby. Then another. They were even more deadly than the wave.

The water poured into the Palace through every archway and balcony, filling rooms and hallways, falling down staircases. The white foam sprayed the walls, stealing the paintings from their place. It tore down anything in its path; curtains, chairs, servants, walls. The ocean broke pillars, ceilings came crashing down, sending enormous waves in every direction. It churned, leaping like a living thing down halls and into rooms, gathering everything in its way. It yearned for destruction. It crashed through the doorway into a bedroom. Circling around the room, it collected anything it could, slamming it into the walls and floor before dragging it along. A woman screamed for her life as the ocean surged around her bed, picking it up and smashing it against the wall. It poured into the King's chambers, swooping up every pillow and stone dove. It ripped every tapestry from the wall, every scroll from its shelf. It thundered into the kitchens, catapulting food from the tables it devoured. It chased after cooks and servants as they tried escaping the ocean's wrath. It doused the fires, spilled the soups, and emptied the cupboards of their dishes. The raging sea poured from the doorways leading to the garden, down the staircases, eager to join in the terror of the village.

Underground the Equalizers were dying fast. Most still left alive had the same idea as Bacillus. In almost every tunnel water was destroying walls. Each time a sorcerer pushed the water out of the tunnel he was in, it would take away the walls support, and the whole tunnel would collapse. All around the island, sink holes opened up, in the

Trune's realm and in the villages. One of the largest opened up right below the Palace. The Equalizers were destroying Atlantis, and it was costing them their lives.

✳✳✳

Philo and Nicky had just climbed the last stair when the entire Palace shuddered.

"What was that?" Nicky asked. The two friends looked down the hall.

"Nicky if we don't make it out of this," Philo's hand was on her shoulder.

"Philo..." she saw him looking into her eyes. She did not know what to say. Suddenly the entire hall shifted steeply to the left. Nicky screamed as she fell, sliding rapidly down the incline. Philo had just managed to grab the doorway, his outstretched hand just barely missing Nicky's. With a cry Nicky grabbed onto another doorway. She watched as the paintings and vases leapt to their doom, shattering and smashing against the wall that was now the floor.

"Nicky!" Philo yelled down to her. He had gotten back into the staircase and was peeking his head around the wall. "Nicky! Try to climb into the room!"

Nicky looked up at the doorway she was clinging to. Carefully, she struggled into it. Finally, she was able to swing her leg into the doorway and was safe. Glancing into the room she realized it was another hallway. A huge crack was in the floor, walls and ceiling. She peeked out to look up at Philo. He was about to say something when a huge noise overpowered his speech. He turned to look behind him, up the hallway. Flying towards them were thousands of gallons of water. Before Philo could react he was swept down with it, plummeting down past Nicky.

She screamed, covering her ears as the water thundered past her. Suddenly the Palace shifted again, and water came flying at Nicky. She was thrown violently down the hall way, approaching the crack. The part of the hallway she was in began to fall downward. By the time she reached the crack it was three feet above her. She was slammed against the large chunk of stone. Water piled above her head. She jumped up, pushing as hard as she could with her feet. She managed to get her arms over the floor of the hallway on the other side and pulled herself up. The water helped slightly as it was falling towards her. She struggled for several long seconds before she was free. She ran, fast, down the hall. A huge vibrating groan ricocheted down the hall through Nicky's very being. She spun around just in time to see the part of the Palace she was just in drop. She turned and ran down another hall. Behind her, water tore through the open archways, pummeling down the tilted hall after her, careening over the marble floor. It swept over a vase of flowers, slamming it against the ground. Compared to the roaring water, the breaking glass did not make a sound.

She ran harder. Nicky could barely hear a thing, the churning water filling her ears. She made a sharp right into a room, hoping to escape the water. It rushed into the room after her, flying around her ankles faster than she could even imagine. It knocked her off her feet and swallowed her whole before she could take a breath. The water swirled around her, pushing her down, spinning her. She squeezed her eyes shut, flailing her arms as she was pulled into the erratic current. The wave flew up the wall, taking her with it. In a few precious seconds she was above water. She gasped for breath just before she went back under. She had lost all sense of direction. Up was left and down was backwards and forward was upside-down. She felt the floor beneath her and pushed off, only to find it was the wall. She was yanked from the room and was propelled down a staircase. There was so much water that she did not even touch the stairs. At the bottom of the staircase she was heaved against the wall. She hit her head and everything went dark.

Uncertainty

Slowly, Nicky regained consciousness. She groggily opened her eyes. What happened? Where was she? She tried looking around but everything was blurry and nothing made sense. Something was drifting by her to the left, other items were spinning quietly in place. As Nicky's senses began to clear she could feel something pressing against every part of her, like air only stronger. She reached up and touched her forehead. Not only did her head feel funny, but her hand did as well. She held it in front of her face. Gradually her hand came into focus. It seemed alright. She spread out her fingers. Stretched between every finger was a thin, translucent membrane of skin. She closed her eyes and shook her head; her mind must still be fuzzy. She opened her eyes and looked around the room. Things were starting to become more clear. Flowers floated all around the room, close to the ceiling. Around her a few pillows drifted by. By now she was able to focus, and suddenly, she realized that she could not feel the floor beneath her. She rapidly spun her head down to look at the tile. As she did she felt the rest of her body twirl around to face the floor. She was about four feet off the ground. She was instantly confused and frightened. What was going on? Was she dead? Is that why she was floating? It was at this moment that she realized that she could not feel her legs.

She spun around to look at them. There, instead of two long legs, there was one very long, dark blue fish tail. She screamed, kicking ferociously to try to escape the thing that was attached to lower body. She hastily swatted at it, trying to get rid of it. She continued screaming as she flew into the wall, hard. Her dress billowed up around her. She batted it away, not letting the tail thing out of her sight. That did not stop her screaming, in fact it made it louder as she bounced off the wall and began hurtling towards the ceiling. Suddenly Philo sped into the room.

"Nicky! Stop!" he grabbed her arms, trying to keep her in place. She continued to panic, kicking and swiping at the tail, causing both of them to spin in circles.

"What's going on?" she shouted, eyes wide.

"Nicky! Calm down!" Philo held her arms tightly. She continued to struggle.

"Nicky!" He grasped her chin, forced her to look into his eyes.

She stared at his green eyes, then into them, absorbing his calmness. Slowly, her breathing slowed to normal.

"Okay," Philo slowly let go of her.

Nicky's dress was twirling around her waist. She pulled it back down to where her knees should have been as she took in her surroundings. They were floating in the upper corner of the room. It slowly dawned on her that everything was floating around the room, except heavier things. With a start she realized that everything was under water.

"Are you hurt?" Philo asked.

Nicky tentatively shook her head. "Philo, what—"

"Do you remember how we were telling the sorcerers about different spells they could do based on what outcome the prophecy had?"

Nicky nodded her head.

"Remember how one of the spells was to turn everyone into a fish?"

Realization slowly came across Nicky's face.

"Well, they were trying to do that when the wave overpowered Fidus. The spell was only half done, so everyone is half fish."

"What?" Nicky could not believe it, yet she had to. She carefully looked down to where her feet should have been. She saw a long, flowing fin at the end of a slender tail. She looked at Philo. He was also part fish. His tail was dark green. Both their fins waved gently back and forth, keeping pace with the other, keeping them stationary.

"What does this mean?" she asked.

Philo shook his head. He did not know either.

Suddenly Nicky gasped. "Where's Father?"

"He's fine."

"Really?"

"He's alive, he's okay."

"But the prophecy—"

"I know, I can't figure it out either."

"Do you know where he is?"

Philo nodded and motioned Nicky to follow. He turned and slowly propelled himself out the door, swimming like a dolphin, looking back at Nicky expectantly. Nicky followed, clumsily at first but figuring it out fairly quickly. Outside, the hall was littered with shattered vases, sand, paintings and debris that was once their Palace ...

"Philo! Why is there water everywhere?" It had just occurred to her to ask.

"The Palace sank into the ocean," he replied. "I don't know how, but you look out the window and it's the seafloor."

He was right. Nicky swam to an archway in the hall that had once had a view of the village but now looked out on a patch of seaweed.

As they continued swimming, Nicky realized that they were near the ceiling. She looked down at the floor, a remnant of a hallway she had walked down many times. When she had walked it felt friendly, close, and familiar. Now, swimming up by the ceiling

it looked huge, distant, alien. Fear tightened around
her chest. She did not know why exactly, but being
up so high scared her. She quickly swam down so
that she was swimming only a few feet from the floor.
Philo followed her example. She looked at the walls,
the floors, the shattered possessions strewn across
the hall. What had been so full of life now was like
going through ancient ruins. Nicky had only done
that once, with a few other children years ago. Before
Atlantis became a kingdom, they were just a group of
villages, all living as they liked in what later became
the Tem 's realm. When Atlantis became a kingdom,
everyone moved to a more open part of the island,
and the previously populated village fell to decay.
When Nicky and the other children had gone, moss
and spiders had taken over. While some of the
children had loved it, Nicky felt as if she was walking
into a closely guarded sanctuary and someone would
discover them at any moment. To her, it was as if
strange, eerie people still lived there, even though it
was obvious no one did. Nicky got so scared that she
never went back. She felt that way now, gliding
silently through her own halls and stairways. Just
yesterday the halls were full of light, and a soft
breeze would blow through the open archways. Now
there were only shadows and a dark muckiness.

Nicky was not very far behind Philo but she raced
to catch up with him. He reassuringly reached for
her hand, which s took gratefully. They swam this
way, hand-in-hand, down the stairways and through
broken rooms, until they reached a part of the wall
that was completely destroyed, a gaping hole peering
into a dark murkiness. Philo lead Nicky out of the
ruins and swam into the open ocean. The ocean was
in the Palace as well as out, but Nicky considered
them two different places. The moment they had left
the Palace behind them, Nicky looked down. It was if
they had jumped off the tallest balcony and had
stayed suspended in midair. The ocean floor looked

as if it was miles below. Nicky gasped and held onto Philo as if her life depended on it.

"Whoa, hey, it's okay. We can't fall because we're under water." He had both arms around her now, just as Nicky's arms were around him.

She looked around and had never felt so small. She had always felt small as a child, but not like this. As she studied the ocean all around her she imagined it pressing in on her, squishing her as small as she could go until she ceased to exist. She buried her head in Philo's shoulder. They stayed there, suspended in the same place, for a few minutes. Every moment Philo enjoyed, feeling Nicky pressed against him like that, and he hated himself for it. There she was, scared senseless and clinging to him for help and comfort, and all he could think about was his silly crush on her. He took hold of her shoulders and held her at arm's length, for her sake.

"Nicky, listen to me. I know this is new, and different, and scary. But we can get through this. Now let's go see your father."

She nodded and allowed herself to be led by Philo to the seafloor. As they got closer Nicky realized they were headed to a village, or what had been a village. The houses had crumbled, the marketplaces were destroyed, and the brand new cobblestone roads were hidden in the sand, shells, and debris. Right in the center of the village, a spot that had been completely reduced to rubble, was a crowd of people. It looked as if every person who lived in Atlantis was there.

They swam up to join the crowd. Each person looked scared, some looked angry, others confused. They swam around the crowd to the person speaking. It was Rus Nevik, surrounded by most of the other sorcerers. Nicky cast a glance at Philo. Where was her father? The expression on Philo's face said that he did not know either. He quietly moved to a sorcerer near the back.

"Excuse me, where is the King."

The sorcerer turned to answer when his eyes fell on Nicky. He sighed deeply with relief and muttered a prayer of thanks.

"Thank goodness you're alive, Princess." He turned to Philo. "The King is down in the medical ward," he said, pointing to one of the few buildings below that appeared to be intact.

Philo thanked him and swam down, keeping his hold on Nicky's hand.

"Is he alright?" she asked Philo. "Is Father okay?"

"I'm sure he is. When I was found in the Palace I was brought out here with the others. He was talking to everyone, reassuring them and so forth."

They reached the medical ward, a large building that had probably been a silversmiths shop. Just as they reached the doorway a man swam out.

"May I help—" He noticed Nicky, "Princess! Come in, follow me. Oh, and the sorcerer's put a spell over the room, so careful swimming in."

He swam through the doorway, keeping low to the ground. Philo and Nicky followed his example. When they had entered the room they realized why. Inside was only two feet of water, the rest of the open space was air. Philo instantly surfaced, while Nicky slowly raised her head out of the water. At first everything was blurry, but then something slid away from her eyes and she could see clearly. She tried to keep her dress in order but it insisted on swirling around her. She was just thankful her belt was still secure, keeping the bodice in place.

"Oh, my word," Philo breathed from next to her. He was looking right at her.

"What?" she turned to him, droplets sliding down her face.

He leaned in, studying her eyes, his wet hair clinging to his head. Something was off about him but she could not figure out what. She leaned back. "What are you doing?"

"It looked like you had extra eyelids," he stated.

"Excuse me?"

"Here, watch me," he closed his eyes and slid below the water. He opened his eyes and slowly reappeared. Nicky gasped as she saw a single clear eyelid slide away sideways when he was above water. She dunked her head and came back up, eyes wide open.

"Aha! We *do* have extra eyelids now," he thought about something. "That's probably why we can see so well underwater."

Suddenly Nicky knew what was weird. "Philo your voice is *way* higher pitched!"

"What?" as he said it both realized Nicky was right. "What's going on? My voice has already changed."

Nicky shrugged and said, "I don't know." She froze when she noticed her voice was higher as well. "What's happened?" she squeaked.

The two stared at each other, then dove underwater.

"How do I sound?" they both asked simultaneously. "Normal," they responded. They both resurfaced.

"I guess sounds are different under water," Philo said.

"That's right," a sorcerer, Trill Vowtiz, had swam up next to them. "Now both of you please follow me." He swam down the hall that they were in, using primarily his arms to pull himself along. Philo and Nicky followed into the next room.

Inside were rows of people on raft-like beds floating on the water. Some had various parts of them wrapped in bandages and were lying flat, others were sitting up and being examined by doctors or sorcerers. They continued on into a back room.

King Neptus sat on a raft next to a sorceress who was bandaging his arm. His robe was torn away in many places and he looked in need of rest and a warm meal.

"Father!" She swam to him and nearly leapt into his arms.

"Nicky!" It took the sorceress holding him back to keep him from diving in to embrace Nicky.

"Sire, your bandage will get wet," she informed him.

Trill Vowtiz helped Nicky onto the raft next to Neptus. She wrapped her arms around him so tightly she threatened to never let go. He did the same with the unbound arm.

"Oh, Father, I'm so glad you're alive! The prophecy said that you would die and I thought for sure that you would, oh I'm so happy that it was wrong," she would have gone on like this for quite some time if Neptus had not interrupted her.

"Nicky, you're safe! When they didn't find you right away I was so worried." By now the sorceress was done wrapping the King's wound and he placed both arms around his daughter. The sorceress, who was Quen Anrym, eased herself off the raft, swam over to Nicky's side, and hopped back on.

"Sire, I'll need to examine her now," she said softly.

Neptus sighed sadly and let go. Nicky grasped his hand firmly.

"Why do I need to be examined? I'm not hurt,"

"You don't know that for certain," Anrym said. "Wounds look differently underwater."

Quen Anrym then began examining Nicky like she was a new species, which, she found out later, she was. First the sorceress looked at her eyelids. Taking her fingers on one hand, she opened Nicky's eyes wide, and with the other, she slid the clear eyelid back and forth. She let go and Nicky blinked. Next she examined her neck. She began running her fingers what felt like right through Nicky's neck.

"What are you doing?" she demanded.

"Checking your gills."

"My *what?* I have *gills?*"

"Of course. How do you think you were able to breath underwater?"

So much had happened to Nicky in such a short amount of time that she had honestly not thought about breathing.

Once her gills seemed to be in order, the Quen pushed her flat against the raft and began poking her belly.

"Shouldn't a doctor be doing this?" Nicky asked.

"All the doctors are busy tending to people with injuries far greater than yours. Besides, the sorcerers cast the spell to change you, not the doctors."

The Quen had Nicky sit up and examined her hands, focusing on the translucent membrane between her fingers. Nicky took the time to study the Quen's gills, trying to see what the ones on her neck looked like. They looked just like a fish's.

"So what happened?" Nicky looked right at Quen Anrym.

The sorceress sighed, but did not answer, choosing instead to concentrate on Nicky's arm. Nicky studied her skin along with the Quen and realized that her entire body was covered with tiny, fan shaped, flexible scales. Nicky ran her hand over her belly down to where her knees would have been. It felt smooth, not rough like she thought it would.

"Why is my tail blue but the rest of my body normal skin color?"

Anrym shook her head. "I don't know."

"But you said that it was the sorcerers who made the spell."

"I know, but we don't know what happened." She looked at Nicky, then turned to look King Neptus and Philo. She took a breath and began. "When we were on the balcony we started a spell that would turn us all into fish. Someone had brought up that, if we were all fish, we wouldn't be able to turn ourselves human again. But there was no time, we had to do what would save the most people.

"We also knew that we didn't want anything like this to happen again, that we couldn't have anyone disloyal to our king, so we started to create a spell that would only affect those who followed King Neptus."

"I didn't know that was possible," the King breathed.

"We hadn't even executed the spell yet when the wave hit. We shouldn't even be alive right now. But right before we went under, I thought I felt something, Someone more powerful than all of us combined, take over the spell and make it work." She shook her head in wonder. "There's no way any of us would have thought of all this detail. Maybe we could have thought to turn everyone part fish, possible we could have thought of this membrane between our fingers," she held up her hand, "but the other eyelid so that we can see better underwater, or to put scales on our entire bodies, or to have both lungs and gills, I don't think we would have thought of those."

Silence. The people in the room were deep in thought, trying to make sense of this story.

"So, what are you saying happened?" Philo asked.

"All I'm saying, is that Someone far more powerful than every sorcerer I've ever known combined had mercy on us, and gave us the help we needed to survive."

They settled into silence again, the only noise was the water gently rippling against the raft. The Quen went back to examining Nicky. She found a small bump on her head, which she determined was not harmful, and let her down from the raft with only a few scrapes and bruises, nothing even worth bandaging. A few minutes later a large cut was found on Philo's tail near the fin, which was bandaged as soon as he was moved to his own raft in the first room with the others. Nicky had stayed with her father.

"I'm fine," he insisted as they tied cotton to the injury. Of course, the doctors wrapped up the cut anyway. After they had left, Philo let his head drop against the raft. He had been told to lay there without getting the bandage wet. So, of course, he was bedridden. *They're being overly careful,* Philo complained silently.. *They're worried about sharks I bet. I know when there's danger around, I can take care of myself.* No matter how much he sulked, he was still stuck on the raft until the cut healed or a sorcerer healed him. *It's not even that bad.*

Just then a sorcerer swam rapidly through the doorway. "We found him."

Three other sorcerers quickly swam up to him, bringing an empty raft. Behind the first sorcerer was another, dragging someone through the water. Philo sat up, trying to see who it was. They pushed the person onto the raft, steadying it as it rocked slightly. They tried to center him on the raft and he groaned loudly. With a start Philo recognized the man.

"Fidus!"

The man moved his head in response to the name but moaned in pain. The sorcerers quickly pushed him into another room.

With a grunt of determination Philo followed, using his arms to propel the raft forward.

They guided the raft Fidus lay on into the room with Neptus and Nicky.

"Who's that?" Nicky asked.

"It's Fidus," Philo answered as he rowed himself into the room.

"Philo, I told you to stay put," Anrym muttered.

"You said to not leave the raft, and I haven't. Now let me see him!"

One of the sorcerers waved his hand in Philo's direction and a current suddenly appeared below his raft, pushing him away from Fidus, towards Nicky and her father. Philo folded his arms in protest but did not try to get closer.

Four of the sorcerers jumped onto Fidus' raft and began examining him all at once. Two of them, who were masters of healing, ran their hands over him, sensing for anything wrong with him.

"His right arm is broken."

"His left wrist is broken as well."

"He has nearly no energy."

"The left hip is bleeding."

The sorcerer went on like this, reporting anything they found broken or injured, all the while Fidus would groan. One of the sorcerers pressed his hand onto Fidus' forehead, giving him a little energy and relieving some pain.

Three doctors came in, each carrying medical supplies. They put Fidus' arm and wrist in splints, wrapped his wounds, and gave him additional energy, a little at a time. Someone brought in food. Neptus, Nicky, and Philo were all given some, but Fidus had to be fed.

When the sorcerers had done all they could, one stayed with him while the rest went to tend to others. One came to Philo, removed the bandage, and healed the cut.

"Thank you."

After the sorcerer had left Nicky said, "But I still don't understand—"

The sorcerer by Fidus asked for quiet.

"Why don't you two go talk to the other sorcerers?" Neptus whispered. "They might be able to answer questions."

"But Father—"

"I'll be perfectly fine. Besides, I would really like to rest. It's... been a trying day."

Nicky nodded and kissed her father on the cheek. He kissed her and she left with Philo.

They swam through the village in silence. Nicky still could not quite grasp everything that had happened, but a few things rang clear in her mind. For one, her father was safe. She did not understand how, the prophecy had clearly said his reign would end. They would ask the sorcerers and everything would be sorted out. They slid gracefully through the water near the seabed, sand swirling around their tail fins as they moved. Everything was dark, submerged in dark blue shadow. She knew that something menacing was lying in wait, hidden in the darkness. The village was grey, empty, lifeless. Her hand ran along the one standing wall of a house, the rough clay crumbled against her fingertips. She held back tears, realized no one would see them, and let them noiselessly join the surrounding ocean. Her vision quickly became blurry. With dismay she realized that the tears must be trapped behind her new eyelids. She stopped where she was, sinking to the sand and holding on to whatever was left of a shop. She let out a short sob. Everything was lifeless and blurry and she was cold. She wrapped her arms around herself, bowing her head, wanting this to be a nightmare and not reality.

She barely noticed Philo taking hold of her hand and pulling her along. She gradually became aware that she was being taken to the surface, everything was getting brighter and the warmer. She tried to wipe her eyes but of course that did nothing. When they emerged from the water her eyelids lifted and the tears fell freely.

"Where are we going?" she surprised herself with her steady voice.

"To the one part of the island that didn't sink."

She glanced ahead. In the distance was a small cluster of hills sticking out of the water. They reached them fairly quickly.

"The mountains..."

"Yes. Remember how tall they were?"

"They're just hills now," she said sorrowfully. The mountains had been so tall that she could see them from the village, even though they were on the others side of the island.

Philo paddled to the peak raised above of the water. His shoulders fell beneath the waves, then he leapt out of the water, landing on the dry ground. It was not very steep so Nicky chose to climb up. It was different not using legs, but her tail was strong and helped her push her way up. An image of a caterpillar flashed through her mind. She pushed the image away, collapsing on the rocks in a puddle of water and wet clothing. Slowly the chill left her limbs as the warmth seeped into her body.

She rolled onto her back, her eyes closed, her hands folded across her belly, warm from the sun, absorbing the heat, dress almost dry, her tail fin slowly being pulled back and forth by the water. A sort of peace settled over her. Thoughts of the prophecy and Atlantis tried to creep into her mind but she kept them away.

Right now, she wanted nothing more than a calm after the storm.

Resolve

Nicky opened her eyes. She had not realized she had fallen asleep until she woke up. She was looking at the sky, filled with white clouds. Her back and shoulders were sore, probably from the rock she was laying on. Heat seemed to radiate from her arms and face but it felt good. She rolled over onto her belly, her hands folded under her head. Her dress was still a little damp on her back. A warm breeze blew by her, taking her hair and making it dance around her face and shoulders.

"Are you awake?"

She looked up at Philo through golden strands of hair. He was sitting a little farther up the hill about an arm span away.

"How do you feel?" He asked.

"Better. I'm not cold anymore."

"That's good." Unable to think of how to continue the conversation, he turned away.

Nicky sat up. "So, what exactly happened? I mean, this was obviously the prophecy but not everything came true."

"It must have, just not in the way we thought it would. Do you remember it?"

Nicky shook her head. "Not all of it. I remember the first line, *'Conquered by enemy that had once been friend, the king's reign will come to an end.'* The enemy was Bacillus."

"Or the water," Philo added. "What about the King's reign?"

Again, Nicky shook her head.

"We could go see if any of the scrolls are still intact," Philo suggested. "Are you ready to go back?"

She studied the still, sparkling water before her. *"Although life will seem to disappear, Atlantis subjects will still be here,"* she quoted.

Philo's question still hung in the air. She nodded, and they both dove in. She expected the water to be cool against her skin, but for some reason it was not.

"Philo—"

"I know, it's warm," he interjected. Nicky could almost see the answer fly through his head. "What if we're somehow keeping some of the heat from the sun? As in, absorbing it like cloth absorbs water?"

Nicky shrugged. "I believe it. I've seen stranger things today."

Philo laughed. Not mean or sarcastic, but a genuine, joy-filled laugh.

"Why the laughing?"

"Us being turned partly into fish! How are we going to survive?"

Nicky was taken aback by the eagerness in his voice. "Isn't that question supposed to be asked with worry and not excitement?"

"Oh, Nicky, don't you see? It's a challenge! We have to completely change our lifestyle!" he began listing things off with his fingers. "We're probably going to be fishermen now, no more farming. We might find something to harvest, like clams and such, so we'll be gatherers as well. We might want to relocate to a more shallow area, so we can build rafts or hills to lay on so we can absorb heat. Also, cotton clothing is not going to work out, based on my shirt and your dress now having a mind of their own. Let's see, Woven seaweed might work, or maybe skin from some kind of sea creature. And how do we clean fish? Underwater won't be very good, so do we eat on land? I could go on and on, our lives are going to be so much better!"

Nicky was shocked. "Philo, how can you say that? Our city is in crumbles, people are dead or seriously injured, we're not even human," desperation was evident on her face. "How can our lives be *better*? We were safe, we were happy, we were prosperous! Now we're in danger, scared, and have next to nothing. I don't even know how many of my family survived. Remember? Quen Anrym said that the spell only worked on those still loyal to my father. The rest of my family live in other kingdoms with their own kings and queens. Most of my family *are* those other kings and queens. There's no way that they're loyal to my father."

Philo seemed to have lost his excitement, or if he did not he hid it very well. "Follow me."

He swam to the village, Nicky close behind. They soon came upon a group of villagers. Philo asked them where the sorcerers were and was directed to another building. As they swam through the doorway they realized that air was trapped within, identical to the medical ward. There, in the middle of the room, they found five apprentices sitting on rafts surrounded by paper.

"Princess Nickisha," they bowed and continued working.

Nicky and Philo swam closer. One apprentice sitting near them grabbed a dripping wet scroll and ran his hand over it. Water seeped out of the paper and into his hand. He quickly returned the water to the ocean around him and gave the scroll to the apprentice next to him. This apprentice studied the scroll and repaired the writing as best she could. When completed, the scroll was set on another raft. The other three apprentices were doing the same. Nicky looked at a completed scroll, careful not to touch with her wet hands.

"Where are the scrolls from?"

"The Palace, mainly," one of the apprentices answered. "Mostly documents the sorcerers and scribes have kept."

"We're having trouble finding them all," another added. "When the wave rushed through it carried a lot of important papers with it."

"Did you have one of the prophecy?

"I just saw that," a girl near them murmured, looking through her stack of scrolls. She rummaged through, nearly toppling part of the pile back into the water.

"Why don't the sorcerers keep all the water out? That way you wouldn't damage any more papers," Nicky asked.

"Good idea," the girl replied, "Except that now we're—"

"We're fish," Nicky finished.

"Believe me, I still don't quite believe it," the girl added. "Here, I'm pretty sure this is it." She handed it to Nicky, but only after magically drying off the princess's hands.

Leaning on the raft as to not risk the scroll getting wet again, Nicky read through it.

"This is it. Not our scroll, but this is the prophecy."

Philo looked over her shoulder.

Nicky pointed to the first line. "The enemy that had once been friend was Bacillus."

"Actually," one of the apprentices spoke up, "the wave wasn't in the Equalizer's control when it hit us. The enemy is the water."

"Okay then," Nicky continued, "*His family will meet, all but one, for she will see a quivering sun'* was my family and I saw the sun quiver through the wave."

Philo pointed to the third line. "*Much will crash without sound, and some will fall yet hit no ground.'* The water prevented us from hearing anything crash or letting us fall to the ground."

"*From this disaster will come a tale, one handed down without a fail.'* We'll definitely have a story to tell."

"What? Let me see that," the girl said, taking the scroll. "Oh, you're saying tale, as in story, because of the way it's written. Did anyone tell you that when prophecies are heard that the words could mean different things?"

"It might have been mentioned."

"When Teneo heard the Oracle say tale he immediately thought story. But obviously she meant tail," she held her tail out of the water, waving her fins and giggling.

There was a pause as she handed back the scroll.

"Amazing," Philo finally said. "Of course. There's no way we could have seen that." He laughed a little. "It will be a lot easier to pass down this kind of tail. Our kids will be fish, too, I guess."

Nicky smiled and continued reading.

"*Although life will seem to disappear, Atlantis subjects will still be here.* From the surface it looks like Atlantis is gone, when in reality we just live underwater now—"

"Hey Nicky!" Philo interrupted. "This says the King's reign. What if it really means rain? As in water?"

"What do you mean?"

"Remember the contraption he was working on to water crops? The water fell out of pipes and dripped onto the plants! Like rain!"

"The King's *rain.* So Father can still be king?" she asked excitedly.

"Sounds like it," an apprentice interjected, not looking up from the scroll he was drying out.

Nicky dropped the scroll on the raft, spread out her arms, and fell back into the water laughing. She came up saying, "Yes! Yes! Father doesn't die and I don't have to take the throne! Oh, this is wonderful!"

Philo looked at her strangely. "You don't want the throne?"

"Not right now, I'm not nearly ready. I was really worried I would have to take control of a devastated kingdom with distraught villagers. If my father had died, I'd be grieving, so there's no way I could have done it."

"Well, you'd always have us, I mean, your friends and the sorcerers," Philo replied.

"That's true."

"Are you going to keep reading the prophecy?" an apprentice asked impatiently.

"Yes, of course," Nicky turned her head from Philo to the scroll. "Let's see, '*The city will crumble yet not decay, if the sorcerers can find a way.*' The sorcerers could do what they did with this room, trapping air inside, to the rest of the village."

"Another interpretation could be that a village decays if no one lives in it," Philo added. "The sorcerers found a way to save our lives, so the city won't decay."

"Yes, that works too."

"What's the last line?" multiple apprentices asked. Nicky looked up and noticed that all five were listening.

"*All will lie on them to mend, assisted by enemy that is now friend.*"

"Mend our way of life?" Philo suggested.

"Fidus is obviously the enemy that turned friend," Nicky added, "so, I'm thinking that he helps with ideas on how to return to a relatively normal life."

"Nicky, we're not going to return to a normal life down here," Philo stated. "Not like what we had on land. However, we can and will create a new normal."

"So, we're not *returning* to normal, we're *recreating* normal."

"Sounds about right," he smiled. "It will work out, just have faith."

****

The sorcerers all got together to plan. Daily life in Atlantis had severely changed, and they needed to adjust. They created a list of everything that had to be considered. Among other things, the list included obtaining enough food, clothing, sleep, staying warm, and protection against sea predators.

There was an enormous debate on food. Some said that since they were fish themselves, they should not eat fish anymore. Others said that fish ate fish all the time, so it was not an issue. Those who refused to eat fish found a vast supply of edible sea grasses and algae. The rest of the population that continued to eat fish sent out hunting parties. They wove seaweed into immense nets and were able to catch entire schools. A few people started underwater farms of various fish, so as to make food more available. They dedicated the largest trade shops to this task. Others began sea grass farms.

Clothing was a little more difficult. Cotton did not work, everyone could see that. Not only were the cotton bushes gone, but cotton tended to float. It was decided that manta rays and sting rays would be bred for this purpose. Some of the ray could be eaten, but most of it went to clothing. The new attire was tight fitting and smooth, to limit water resistance while swimming.

Mats of sea grass and moss were constructed for beds, along with woven seaweed for blankets. Blankets were not always needed, since the people could now contain heat, but most of them, especially children, felt safer with a blanket.

The mountains were taken apart, the rock and dirt being spread out to create land in greater surface area. Long canals were cut through for accessibility. The people of Atlantis would swim through these canals, find an open spot of land, and lay on it to absorb heat.

Barracudas were the main fear for the people of Atlantis. Nearly as large as they were, they would often ambush solitary villagers. Because of this, Atlantians tended to travel in large groups. The sorcerers cast various spells over the village to keep out anything but Atlantians, but they did not always work. Most villagers whose trade no longer worked underwater, like metal workers and bakers, became watchers, people who swam through the village looking for danger. Philo joined them occasionally.

As Philo said, it would be a challenge to survive, but the people of Atlantis were ready to face it.

It took some time, but over the following months Atlantis fell into a routine.

King Neptus returned order to the people and adjusted quickly. Nicky would sometimes wake up confused and terrified, but she slowly got used to her new life. Not all of the royal family had survived. Some had drowned, but a few were able to return home on salvageable boats. Thankfully, the nearest port was only a few days away. There they replenished their rations, hired new ships, and headed for home.

Fidus was almost completely recovered when he went to live with Philo's family, who had all survived. He was accepted and loved more than he had ever been in his life. Philo even saw him laugh.

It was hard to stay up for the challenge, and all wanted to quit at one point or another, but over all, it was worth it.

Acknowledgements

I thank God, my Lord and Savior. Without whom this book never would have happened.

I want to thank everyone who helped fund this book. Thank you to Kevin Prince, the Broswell family, the Healy family, Allison Prince, the Wrasse family, Allan and Erika Cruz (The Cruzers), Papa and Mimi, Mary Carnegie, Mr. and Mrs. Haller, Travis Mahoney, Eugenia Imandt, Heather Hansen, the Crawford family, Jennifer Cameron, Marisa Potts, the Johnson family, Sarah Sauls, the Davis family, the Lozada family, and the Wojtowicz family. (And it's pronounced Vo-toe-vitch. I think it's German.)

I also want to thank everyone who helped create this book. Thank you Dad, who was always willing to brainstorm at random times of the night, edited everything, and never let me stop for long. (Which, by the way, was a bit annoying. That was some serious writer's block!). Thank you to Mom, who would encourage me to write but, afterwards, shouldn't I be doing math? Thank you to Allison and Cody for never saying it was a waste of time. Thank you to Kaitlyn Hasegawa for reviewing the early chapters and helping with the names. Thank you to Tracy Falk who edited the later draft. Thank you to Mimi, who also edited a few drafts.

And thank you to everyone who bought this book or kept asking when this book would be done so that they could read it! All of you are the best I could ask for.

About the Author

Katelyn Prince was born in Mission Viejo, California, moved to Reno, Nevada when she was a year old, and moved back to California three years later. After nine years she moved back to Nevada, this time to the city of Henderson. She's been homeschooled since first grade and looks forward to homeschooling her kids. She is currently sixteen and lives with her Dad and Mom, Kevin and Tami, and her two younger siblings, Allison and Cody. They have three dogs and two cats. Over the years she has wanted a few different careers, including but not limited to; The President of the United States, a lawyer, a singer, a dancer, a music video script writer, an FBI agent, a detective, an artist, and an author. So far, author is the only one that has gone anywhere. Her parents always got her books on whatever career she was interested in, for which she is very thankful.

Keep up with How the City Fell at
www.HowTheCityFell.com.